CRIME STOPPER KIDS
MYSTERIES

# The Trespasser's
# Unexpected Adventure

D1014398

CRIME STOPPER KIDS
MYSTERIES

# Book One

# The Trespasser's Unexpected Adventure

### The Mystery of the
### Shipwreck Pirates' Gold

# Karen Cossey

Print Version Published by: Stolen Moments (2016)
An imprint of Tui Valley Books Limited.
ISBN: 978-0-473-35967-6 (Softcover)
Kindle Edition First Published by Karen Cossey (2015)
ISBN: 978-0-473-34762-8 (Kindle)
Republished by Stolen Moments
An imprint of Tui Valley Books Limited (2016)
ISBN: 978-0-473-37472-3 (Kindle)

*To*
*Jean and Etheljoy*
*Whose warm friendship and encouragement*
*mean so much to me.*

# Table of Contents

# Chapter One:
# Captain Happy

*Saturday Morning,*

*Summer Half-Term School Holidays*

Logan didn't even look at the sign, let alone read it. He knew what it said off by heart: "Private Property. Keep Out. Trespassers will be Prosecuted". He had always kept out, just like it said, but it was only seven-thirty on a Saturday morning and there was no one around. It was safe to ignore the sign.

Earlier in the week he had spoken with Janet, a friend of his foster parents, who managed Hideaway Lodge, an exclusive retreat for the wealthy. She had told him that no one was staying in the lodge this weekend. It was within walking distance of his home in Cawsand, near Plymouth, so he'd sneaked out early that morning. All he wanted to do was get down to its private beach and check it out for himself. One of the guys at school said there was an awesome as cave down there.

The descent was about sixty feet. He could climb down easily enough—he was pretty good at climbing and he could map out a route from where he was standing. Still, he liked to abseil down, which was why he had taken the gear bag belonging to his older foster brother that morning. Hopefully Cole wouldn't notice it was missing.

Logan pulled out a harness and put it on, then set up an anchor around a sturdy tree. After attaching a holding brake between the anchor and his harness, he threaded his rope through a couple of rap rings, doubling it over at the centre. He wasn't quite sure how long the rope was. It might be a bit short, so he tied a knot in both ends so he wouldn't rappel off it by mistake. After attaching his belay device to the rope he double-checked everything, removed his brake and stepped out backwards over the edge.

He enjoyed the jumping sensation each time he pushed out from the cliff. After all the effort he had taken to set up safely, the abseil down took hardly any time, but the fun of it made the effort worthwhile. He liked any activity with a bit of risk, because if he got hurt, it was his fault—his mistake. He loved the sense of being in control—he had never felt that when he lived with his father.

He had turned thirteen last month and there was nothing from his father. Nothing at all. Not an email or a phone call or anything. Useless. His father had been hopeless his entire life. Why couldn't he have a decent dad? Maybe it was his fault his father was such a loser. Since his birthday it felt like this black cloud had descended round his head and was gripping his shoulders.

But this morning he had left the black cloud on top of the cliff. He was down on the beach and he was going to explore.

He untied himself from the rope and started to hide it behind some branches.

"Don't do that!" A girl's voice sounded behind him. "I want a turn."

Logan groaned as he turned around. "I thought no one was here."

The girl's green eyes sparkled. She leaned forward, looked around, lowered her voice and said, "If you'd come yesterday, no one would have been here, because yesterday my name *was* 'No one'. I was an escaped prisoner from the Mines of Certain Doom and Death, and I didn't want anyone to see me."

She stood up straight and placed her hand on the hilt of a sword tied to her belt. "Today I've got a new name, so please don't call me 'No one'. I'll get my days mixed up, and very bad things happen when I get my days mixed up."

She scowled at him, and then grinned.

Logan screwed up his face as he deciphered this – obviously, he was dealing with an expert at make-believe.

The girl was probably about eleven. She was skinny, with long black hair plaited down her back. She wore shorts and a T-shirt with a pirate bandana on her head and although it was just eight in the morning, she jumped from foot to foot as if the sand was too hot for her. Poet, his younger foster sister, would say the girl was pretty. Not that he ever paid much attention to that kind of thing. Her sword was interesting though—it looked almost real. He could do some damage with that.

"What's your name today?" he asked.

"Captain Happy, of course! The friendliest pirate on all the seas," she said, flourishing her sword, "and I'd be mighty happy if you gave me a turn with that there rope of yours."

She dropped the sword, grabbed the rope out of Logan's hands, and started climbing hand over hand, kicking herself out from the cliff with her feet.

"Hang about Captain Happy—you should have safety gear on!" He started free climbing up after her. She was an incredible climber. He had never seen anyone her age handle a rope so fast and skilfully. There probably wasn't much point going after her, except that if she fell he would be in so much trouble.

"Get down from there. Right now!" a man's voice shouted from below.

Captain Happy froze. A burst of angry Italian exploded from her lips. She swung back down to Logan and paused.

"It's Captain Blackbeard the Destroyer. Don't worry, I've got this. Give him a minute to yell at me, and then come down."

Captain Blackbeard started shouting at her before she reached the ground. "I thought we had a deal. No more climbing unless I'm with you!"

Logan winced. Must be her father. Maybe he should escape to the top of the cliff while he still had time.

"Climb down here, young man, or I'll come and get you. And I'm twice as fast as she is, so don't even think about going up."

Too late! Captain Blackbeard sure sounded stern. If he *was* faster than Captain Happy, Logan had only one choice. He headed down, hoping he could outrun him if he needed to.

When he got down, he stole a few furtive glances at Captain Blackbeard from underneath his fringe. He was a strong-looking man, clean-shaven, with short straight black hair and vivid green eyes, the same colour as Captain Happy's. He almost looked like a movie star, or perhaps an international espionage agent. Hopefully he wasn't carrying a gun.

"You must be Logan," Captain Blackbeard said.

Logan pushed his fringe aside and stared at Captain Blackbeard. He was frowning, though Logan noticed a smile in his eyes.

"Wha ... How'd you know that?" Logan asked.

The frown suffocated the smile out of the man's eyes, so Logan added a respectful, 'Sir'.

"Janet told me. We arrived two nights ago, so I called in on her to check up on a few things. She said there was a young guy who'd wanted to know if anyone was staying this weekend. She figured you were going to come down that cliff looking for the cave."

Logan reddened.

"Snapped!" said Captain Happy, clapping her hands together.

"So, how were you going to explore the cave when you need a rope to climb to it and your only rope is double-knotted and can't be pulled down?" Captain Blackbeard asked.

"Um ..." What an idiot!

There was silence for a full minute. Captain Blackbeard's stare was intense, like a storm cloud full of lightning. Logan dropped his gaze and watched his shuffling feet. Should he run now?

Captain Blackbeard chuckled—Logan looked up. The smile in Captain Blackbeard's eyes now reached down to his mouth, and it felt like the sun had come out.

"Did you not read the sign about trespassers?" Captain Blackbeard asked.

"No, actually, I didn't. I'm really sorry about that."

Captain Happy spoke up in a serious tone, her nose pointing upwards. "It's obvious Captain Cliffhanger here has a moral objection to reading. I suggest we make him walk the plank, and once he's been well and truly mutton-lated by the sharks we give him pancakes till his stomach bursts."

"You mean mutilated," Captain Blackbeard said. "Or, we could do the pancakes first and see if he keeps any treasure in his stomach when it bursts open, then feed him to the sharks."

Captain Happy poked Logan's stomach with her sword.

"What d'ya say, Captain Cliffhanger? Pancakes and sharks with us here pirates, or another boring day at the top of the rope?"

She came close and whispered in his ear, "Don't worry about the sharks. He'll forget all about them after the third pancake."

Logan hesitated, but the look of cheerful expectancy on Captain Happy's face banished his uncertainties away. This could be fun—even if it did mean acting like a silly eleven-year-old.

"The pancakes sound pretty good to me, Captain Happy. But can I ask one thing?" he said.

"You can speak, prisoner," she said, her nose back in the air.

"Why is he called Captain Blackbeard when he doesn't even have a moustache?" He lowered his voice and pretended to look around for danger.

The two Captains looked at each other. "Observant fellow, isn't he?" Captain Blackbeard said. "Make a good spy."

"True," said Captain Happy. She turned to Logan and said, "He's unco-nerdo."

Captain Blackbeard frowned at her. "Incognito," he corrected.

"That too," said Captain Happy. "But don't let the disguise fool you. One angry look from him can fry your organs inside of you, even when it's pouring with rain and snowing on your head."

She clutched her stomach and took a few staggering steps. "You'll die a sudden but agonising death."

That was true, Logan thought. Captain Blackbeard's stare a minute ago had fried Logan's insides for sure.

"But you'll also die smiling, because Captain Happy here makes everyone laugh, even when they're being tortured by having a bulldog clip pegged on their tongue," said Captain Blackbeard. "I suggest we go now before the First Mate gets angry about Janet's pancakes getting cold."

He turned to Logan. "We don't want to make the First Mate angry, or we'll all get thrown to the sharks before we get to eat anything."

"Scary!" Captain Happy trembled before running off. After only a few feet she ran back and pulled on Logan's arm.

"Race ya!" she shouted.

Logan frowned. "But I don't know where I'm going."

Captain Happy was bouncing up and down. "I know, I know! That means you'll have to follow me and I'm sure to win! I never get to beat Captain Blackbeard."

She turned and took off.

Logan laughed and chased after her. Today he was going to forget his problems and have some fun. Perhaps even be ridiculous. It didn't matter—nobody he knew was about, so he could be as silly as he liked. These people were probably only here for the weekend anyway. He would never see them again. He was going to focus on being the best pirate he could be. Or maybe the worst.

Charles Gomander sat on his balcony, looking out at the lake. Only a few more days and he would be wealthier than he had ever dreamed possible. One final delivery from Hideaway Lodge, and he would be able to disappear. No more obnoxious students ignoring him. He could spend the rest of his life visiting the locations he had tried to teach those ungrateful brats about.

As long as it went smoothly, and no one saw what was going on. The men from London were getting anxious about how long this whole covert deal had taken, and how much hard cash it was costing them. Not that they wouldn't get it all back a hundred times over.

Thankfully, he had Oscar and Zach to sort out any problems. They weren't afraid to get their hands dirty, even if it meant spilling a bit of blood. That's what would have to happen to anyone who got in the way now.

It was warm outside, but Charles shivered. He wasn't a murderer, but he knew he wouldn't stand in the way of Oscar or Zach, if that's what they had to do. Not when he was this close to having it all.

# Chapter Two:
# Weapons Training

As Logan rounded a corner after Captain Happy, a castle-like mansion came into view. His foster mum had told him it used to be the summer residence for the lord of the estate many years ago. The estate had been turned into a private park and the house had been modernised and turned into an exclusive retreat for the rich and famous.

All it needed was a moat and Logan would have looked round for knights on horses. Mind you, the swimming pool off to the side was big enough to substitute for a moat. Bet there were no sea monsters in there though, this place looked too tidy for fun like that.

It was set at the back of the secluded cove, surrounded by high cliffs and trees on both sides. The only access, apart from the sea, was a driveway that wound its way down the hill behind the house.

Logan stopped behind Captain Happy. What kind of mysteries had the house hidden over the years? Maybe someone had been taken hostage or even murdered. He smiled at the thought—the place was spotless, but there might be something grisly lurking there.

Captain Happy waved to a woman standing on the terrace. Logan blinked–there was nothing grisly about her. He could tell she was beautiful, even without Poet there to point it out.

"Who's that?" he asked. The woman looked kind of familiar, as if he had seen her somewhere, but no one he knew could afford to stay here.

Captain Blackbeard was standing beside him now. Logan watched him put his hand over his heart. "That, Captain Cliffhanger, is my soul mate."

Captain Happy turned to look back at them both and rolled her eyes. "You mean, First Mate."

"That too," Captain Blackbeard said. "You can call her Ma'am, as all bad pirates would if they wanted to be fed while they were off adventuring. You two had better go over there and wash the sand off your feet while I explain Captain Cliffhanger's perilous punishment."

He winked at Logan and pointed to the outside foot shower, then ran up to the terrace, grabbed the lady around her waist and spun her through the air.

When she landed she came over to meet Logan. She was slim with dark brown eyes and long, dark brown hair that actually shone like those photoshopped shampoo ads. She looked either Italian or Spanish, and her smile reminded him of Captain Happy. Best of all, she seemed more than pleased to have him join them.

Breakfast was a lot of fun, thanks mostly to Captain Happy's antics. After too many pancakes to count, Logan was totally at home.

"Thank you for feeding me. I know I should say I'm sorry for gate-crashing your breakfast, but I'm not. I haven't laughed so much for ages. But I guess I'd better get going now and leave you to your holiday," he said. Shame.

Captain Blackbeard looked at Ma'am, who nodded and smiled.

"Well Logan, er … I mean Captain Cliffhanger," said Captain Blackbeard. "I want you to know, I admire a man who doesn't say sorry unless he means it. I also admire how you called out to Happy here when she, in direct contravention of the rules, started climbing that rope." He glared at Captain Happy with one of his internal organ-burning stares. She looked kind of sizzled as she stared at her hands.

Captain Blackbeard relented and leaned forward, rested his arms on the table and looked Logan straight in the eyes. "Your first instinct was obviously to keep her safe, and a person who looks out for the welfare of others, even pirates, deserves to be commended."

"Really?" Logan wanted to soak up this man's praise. This time Captain Blackbeard's stare seemed to reach right down to Logan's soul as if he was inspecting it. Would he like what he saw? It would be something if he did.

"Really. It shows a basic respect for the value of others, which is not always easy to find these days. I also commend you on your rock climbing. I can see the mountain goat inside of you."

He leaned back in his chair, put his hands behind his head and continued, "I do have to say, though, that you are a horrific runner. How you can let yourself be beaten by an eleven-year-old girl is beyond me. I think unless you have somewhere else you need to be, you should stay here and undergo some serious pirate training for the rest of the day."

Should he object to the running comment? There was that smile in Captain Blackbeard's eyes again.

Logan laughed. "That would be wicked, Captain Blackbeard."

Captain Blackbeard smiled. "Of course it would. We are pirates after all!"

Only for the day though. Who were these people really?

"Are you sure you don't want me to call you by your real name rather than Captain Blackbeard?" Logan asked.

"No. I'm going to keep calling you Captain Cliffhanger, as it is a totally satisfactory pirate name. All pirates leave their old names and lives behind when they take to sea. So you can keep calling me Captain Blackbeard. Tell you what though, let's drop the Captain bit. Cliffhanger, Happy, Blackbeard and Ma'am is what it'll be, just for today. No questions about real names allowed."

Looked like he wasn't going to find out who these people were. Be good to know, but if they didn't want to say, he'd just drop it. He wasn't going to risk offending them, not when he really wanted to stay for the day.

"Do you need to tell someone where you are?" Blackbeard asked.

Logan squirmed in his seat. He should tell the truth—he would hate to upset his foster parents.

"I told my foster dad, Steve, that I was going to the beach for the day and I'd be back by dinnertime. He's a coastguard and is going quite a way out to sea today, so isn't going to be back until then anyway. Abby, my foster mum, is a costume supervisor for the Theatre Royal in Plymouth, and it's their yearly conference in London. She doesn't get back until tonight either. They would want to know if I was going to be at someone's place. They probably won't like me staying without meeting you."

"Well done, Cliffhanger. A pirate who tells the truth even when it could go against him. Excellent. Means you passed the honesty test and are allowed to stay." Blackbeard sure looked pleased. "As it so happens, the reason Janet remembered about you was because Steve was standing right behind me waiting to talk to her. We all had a great chat about you and your shenanigans. In fact, we had a coffee together and talked about all sorts for almost an hour. Seems a premium man, your dad."

Logan's mouth gaped open.

Happy grinned. "Snapped again!"

"Go inside and call him. The phone's by the fridge. We had a bet—I said you wouldn't ignore the trespassing sign, and he said you wouldn't even read it. All you need to do is tell him he was right about the sign, and ask if it's okay to stay until dinner."

Was this for real? Logan went inside and dialled his foster dad's mobile number, hoping he wasn't out of range yet.

"I can't believe you trespassed," said Steve after he'd explained what had happened. "You can stay though. He seemed a decent guy when I talked to him, and Janet said they're a real good sort of people. Have fun—but don't forget to be respectful. Call Cole if you have any problems, otherwise we'll pick you up at dinnertime."

"Let's go to sea then, Blackbeard!" Happy shouted when Logan came outside again.

She jumped around the table then swung her arms around Blackbeard's neck. "We could make a raft out of driftwood, or float in a barrel, or ask the giant seagull of the north to carry us across the waves on his back."

Blackbeard was smiling. "Or we could use the sea kayaks from the shed."

"'Fraid not, me hearties." There was not a trace of fun on Ma'am's face as she looked at Happy.

Happy sighed, "I know, I know, I have to get my bracing sorted before I'm allowed out on the ocean in a kayak."

Logan had only begun lessons in a sea kayak so he needed practice at using his paddle to stop the kayak capsizing as well. Not that he minded tipping—it was kind of fun. Judging by what Blackbeard said next, he figured Happy wasn't quite so confident with capsizing.

"A few more rolls would be a good idea. Never mind, we can still have a good time. How about we go searching for treasure in the cave Cliffhanger's so keen to see?"

"That'd be awesome!" Logan said. This could be the only chance he would ever get to see the cave.

"I guess it could be kinda magnif-ibang," said Happy. "Do we need climbing gear?"

Blackbeard nodded.

"Then let's go, Cliffhanger!" She grabbed Logan by the arm and starting dragging him down the terrace steps.

"I'm going to stay here and take it easy," Ma'am said.

"That's code for have a nana nap. You know, forty winks and snoozeroo time," whispered Happy to Logan, and then covered her eyes with one hand and his eyes with her other hand. "Blurk, kissing. Don't look—you might get poisoned. Would you two cut that out, peeerlease!" she called out to Blackbeard and Ma'am.

Blackbeard let go of Ma'am and jumped off the edge of the terrace to the lawn below. "Race you to the boat shed," he yelled.

He was waiting inside the shed when they got there. It was more like an old done-up house than a shed—it must have cost a packet to fix it up. Blackbeard explained that in the past it had been the grounds man's residence, but now it was used for storage. The kayaks were stacked in a room that had been changed from a living area into a boat room. Leading off from it was an old kitchen that had been modernised into a workshop, and a bedroom lined with shelves stacked with climbing gear and beach equipment. There were a couple of locked doors—must be out of bounds storage cupboards.

Blackbeard held up two backpacks.

"I forgot we brought these, Happy. I suggest we have some weapons training before we wear ourselves out in the cave. You never know who we may need to fight for the treasure."

"That's a blastingly brilliant idea, Blackbeard," Happy said as she took a bag.

"All right then," Blackbeard said. "Girls against boys. Happy, I give you exactly five minutes to wake Ma'am up and strategise, then we're going to come and blow you to smithereens. You won't stand a chance. Synchronise your timepiece, please."

Happy fiddled with her watch then raced inside. Logan flicked his fringe out of his eyes as he blinked at the bag. What had he got himself in for?

"Don't look so anxious, Cliffhanger. I assume all boys your age know how to fire a Nerf gun?" Blackbeard asked.

What? He's got to be kidding!

Logan puffed his chest out. "I am the undefeated king of Nerf gun war."

"Well done. You'll need to be beyond good though. The First Mate is exceptional with a Nerf gun. Well, she's exceptional with most things, except cooking that is. But let's forget that for now and focus on killing her and Happy quickly and cleanly. Here's how I think we should do it."

He outlined a detailed plan that involved lots of hiding behind things and crawling under things and jumping over things. Awesome! The timer on his watch went off and they raced outside.

The back yard turned into the front lines of a warzone, with a tremendous amount of shouting, racing about and Nerf gun darts flying through the air. Logan was doing well of course, but then out from behind a tree sprung Ma'am and somehow pinned him to the ground.

"Gotcha ya ugly piraty scoundrel!" she whooped.

"Don't worry, I've got this," Blackbeard shouted from the same tree. He jumped down and snatched the Nerf gun out of Ma'am's hands. "Stick 'em up—or I'll put a bullet right through that pretty head of yours!"

"You're forgetting one very important thing." Ma'am smiled a wicked-looking grin as she let go of Logan and moved away. Blackbeard looked over to the house and saw Happy standing there, holding a hose.

"Now that's not fair," he said, as he and Logan were drenched with water. Ma'am went and stood beside Happy as Blackbeard held up his hands.

"All right, all right, we surrender."

Rats—that sucked!

"Sorry to let you down, Blackbeard," Logan said as he stood up.

"Don't give up yet, Cliffhanger. The girls hate getting wet. Rush 'em on three. One, two, three."

They both charged. Happy screamed and dropped the hose. Logan grabbed it and turned it on Ma'am while Blackbeard picked up Happy and threw her into the nearby swimming pool, screaming all the way.

"Wicked!" Logan said.

"You like that?" asked Blackbeard, taking the hose out of his hands and pointing it towards the ground, away from Ma'am. "Can you swim?"

Logan thought of the games he played with Poet in the public pool. "Like a piranha sniffing out its prey." The next moment he was flying through the air before coming down with a tsunami of a splash. Superb!

"That was great!" he said to Happy. "Blackbeard must be pretty strong."

"A billion press-ups every morning will do that to you," Happy said as she treaded water. "I really thought we had him that time. It's very disheart-per-turb-u-lating."

"Yes, I can see that by the total disappearance of happy from your face," Logan said as he climbed out of the pool. "But it was also fling-sling-ingly-hurl-some, don't you think?"

Happy's mouth fell open. "For someone with a moral objection to reading, that was an exception-ni-fi-cent word, Cliffhanger. There's hope for you yet."

She climbed out of the pool and sat on the edge next to him. "Now that we're all wet we should go caving, don't you think?"

"How about you two grab a towel and lie on the sand to dry off while I get the gear together," Blackbeard said.

Logan's disappointment must have shown on his face, because Blackbeard spoke again. "Don't worry, Cliffhanger. We will get there, but first I need to make sure we have everything we need to be safe. If you're going to hang from a cliff, I don't want you to fall off. Be most inconvenient."

"He's always worried about being safe," said Happy. "He's a CHAD."

Logan rubbed the back of his neck. "Huh?"

"You know. A Child Hazard Alert Dad. A CHAD. Like this …" She paused then shouted, "'Watch out, don't walk so close to the edge of the footpath! You might fall in the gutter and be swept down the drain to the sea where you'll be eaten by giant bloodsucking jellyfish'. Or, 'Be careful! Make sure you've got your parachute on securely before you go on that swing in case you get knocked off by a passing aeroplane'. Or my favourite, 'Would you stop running down that hill! There might be an earthquake and you won't be able to stop yourself from tripping into a crack and falling right through the earth into outer space!'"

"My foster dad can be like that, too. How about this?" Logan started shouting, "'You can't do cartwheels on the grass—you'll fling killer worms up onto your face and they'll suffocate you with puke-smelling slime until you die! Or, 'Don't touch that excellent climbing tree! You might be captured by squirrels and beaten to a pulp so they can store you for winter food.'"

Happy beamed. "Nasty."

Blackbeard's face tightened until his eyes were narrow slits. He put his hands out and smashed them together as he spoke. "How about, 'Watch out for a pair of big pirate hands banging your heads together'. Or even better, 'Stop hassling the chief captain or you might not be able to go climbing.'"

Happy stood up, smiling a sheepish grin. "I'm going to get that towel."

Logan jumped up, too. "I'll come with you."

In a speedboat, a long way out at sea, two men were both glaring through binoculars as they watched Happy and Logan head inside.

"I thought no one was staying at the lodge this weekend!" Oscar said, his lips flattening as he scowled. He was fierce-looking, covered in tattoos and scars from street fights. He was so large that one angry stomp would capsize the boat.

"Must have turned up unexpectedly," Zach said as he took a step back. He was a shorter man, but with as much the look of a thug as Oscar.

"We can't go moving the loot now, can we? We're gonna hafta keep an eye on em and see when they take off. Maybe Alex can tell us when they're checking out. The bossman's gonna be climbing the wall. We'll miss the pickup if we don't get the last load onshore by Monday. He's gotta make that deadline or he'll lose all his stash. Maybe even his life."

Zach raised his eyebrows. "Would the London big earners really burn him?"

"The boys who bankrolled this whole operation don't take kindly to broken promises. They'd be only too happy to take over the whole scene themselves, even if it meant whacking us all off."

## Chapter Three:
## Questions Asked

Before long Logan and Happy were sitting on the sand, munching on the apples Ma'am had given them.

"Blackbeard's awesome," Logan said.

Happy smiled. "He's a grizzly among teddy bears."

"You're pretty lucky." Logan sighed as his heart started aching. Maybe the black cloud was lurking down here on the beach after all. He shut his eyes—he had to stop the bad weather in his heart.

"But Cliffhanger," Happy said, "Blackbeard said your dad was premium. He must be something to tweet about too."

"That's my foster dad. My real dad's ..." Hot tears welled up in his eyes. Why now? It felt like the angry black cloud that had been threatening to rain since his birthday wasn't going to be pushed away again, no matter how hard he tried.

"He's a humongous jerk. He never even phoned me on

my birthday. All my life he's either just ignored me or yelled at me. He hates me."

Whoa, that sounded way angry! How could he be that hurt over a stupid birthday anyway? He buried his face in his knees, and took some deep breaths. Happy squeezed his shoulder.

"Did he hit you?" Blackbeard asked, appearing out of nowhere. He sat down besides Happy and put his arm around her.

Logan looked up and his back went straight and tight. If only that earthquake crack Happy had talked about would appear underneath him and spew him into outer space. Splat, his whole body would burst to pieces. Maximum grim, but better than being captured by Blackbeard's steady gaze and not knowing how to escape it.

He dug his toes into the sand. "Sometimes. Guess you'll want me to leave now."

Blackbeard's forehead creased. "Why would I want that?"

"I'm a bad influence. If my own dad hits me, I'm not worth having around."

There it was. His blackest thoughts. Followed by a few tears that leaked out the corner of his eyes.

"Logan, it's not your fault your father hit you. I'm sure you've been told that. Don't even go down the 'It's my fault' road. It leads nowhere except into lies and sadness."

"That's what Steve and Abby say," Logan said wiping his eyes, "but lately I can't shake the thought that it *is* all my fault. If only I'd been different somehow, not such a disappointment, he might have loved me better!"

There, it was all out. Now what would Blackbeard say?

Blackbeard was shaking his head. "Logan, it's your father's fault he doesn't love you right, not yours. Any man can become a father, but not every man is capable of being a good dad. Some people simply have no idea how to look after their kids. It's your dad's problem, his fault, not yours."

Logan stared back at him, picking up every word and examining them. For the first time since his birthday, some hope pierced through the black cloud. But the next words out of Blackbeard's mouth squashed the hope dead.

"Look at your foster dad. I'm sure he loves you—he sounded proud of you when we spoke. If it was your fault your dad didn't love you, your foster dad wouldn't be able to love you, either."

Logan felt the watery smile that had been sloshing around his face take a dive.

"What is it? Why the sad face when I talk about Steve?" asked Blackbeard.

Logan mumbled and stared at his shuffling feet kicking up the sand. Why couldn't Blackbeard just drop it? Build a sandcastle or something. Anything!

"Out with it, Logan."

Logan gave a big sigh. "Sometimes I don't feel like I belong with my foster dad and mum."

Blackbeard looked puzzled, so Logan sighed again and continued. "You see, I was friends with their son, Nate. The first time he came around to my place, my dad was drunk and threatened to hit me."

Logan shivered. He had been so scared his dad was going to hit him in front of Nate. Or worse, that he might hit Nate. He shook his head and the picture disappeared.

"Nate grabbed me and dragged me to his place. He told Steve I had to stay with them from now on. So it's not like Steve had a choice. He's a decent guy—he wouldn't have sent me back. But how can I know if he and Abby actually want me around? I wasn't their choice—I was pushed on them."

"Have you asked them?"

"No. I don't know how."

"You know Logan, Steve sure acted like he loved you and thought of you as his son. But you need to take some of that courage you have for stepping out over the edge of a cliff and use it to talk to him and Abby. It's the only way you'll know for sure."

Blackbeard looked like he cared. Maybe this whole thing with his foster parents did matter. Maybe *he* mattered. He smiled as the hope returned, giving him some warmth inside where before there'd only been coldness. Perhaps his black cloud might turn into a rainbow one day soon.

"Okay. Maybe I will," he said.

Blackbeard studied his face, and then at long last, stopped looking at him. They were quiet for a few minutes, watching the waves.

"Do you know why the ocean makes all that crashing noise?" Happy asked. She kept talking, not waiting for a reply. "It's crying because people come and put their sad in it. It's got all the sad of all the people in the world all swallowed up inside it."

She looked at Logan. "You've got big sad eyes, Cliffhanger. When I look in them, I can see down to the bottom of your heart."

She cupped her hands over his eyes.

"What are you doing?" Logan asked.

"Taking the sad from your heart and throwing it in the ocean."

She put her cupped hands together and walked down to the water. Logan followed her.

When she got in up to her knees, she bent down and washed her hands in the waves.

"There, all gone," she said.

Logan stared at the water. "I still feel a little sad."

"That's the sad that's hiding behind your tummy button. You have to wiggle your feet in the water, and it dribbles out your toes."

Logan wiggled his feet. That did feel better—it kind of tickled. He shut his eyes.

Yow! Something had banged hard on his foot. It was Happy, stomping on him!

"What did you do that for!"

"I thought I could make it come out quicker if I pushed it out with my foot. You know, like when you squeeze the toothpaste."

"I don't think it worked." He grimaced. "What I need to do is swing my toes about a bit."

He lifted up his leg and kicked some water into Happy's face. Bulls-eye! She squealed and kicked some back and they started chasing and splashing each other.

A piercing whistle stopped them mid-kick.

"I thought the idea was to dry off?" Blackbeard called as he stood at the water's edge, holding the towels.

"Oops," said Happy.

She ran up to Blackbeard and grabbed a towel, then handed the second one to Logan.

She turned to face the water again, and pointed to something out at sea. "What's that, Blackbeard?"

Blackbeard put his hand over his eye and squinted.

"Someone out there's watching us!" he said and started rummaging in his bag. "I've got some binoculars in here somewhere." He pulled them out and took a look.

"They're leaving," he said, thrusting the binoculars away. There was hardness in his eyes, as though something had sucked up all the fun and laughter from his face and turned it into stone.

Logan twisted his hands together. "Lots of people stop to look at the lodge from out at sea. It's off-limits from land, so it's the only way anyone around here gets to see the place." Why was Blackbeard so upset?

"Come on, Dad. If it was you-know-who they'd have landed by now, and be asking a million questions," said Happy. "They wouldn't just leave."

Blackbeard considered what she said, and then sighed, his face relaxing. "Sorry, Cliffhanger. It's been crazy mad lately and I just hate the thought of losing our peace and quiet. This is one of the few places we can get away from it all. Let's forget it for now. How about we go climbing?"

They headed off, with Logan trailing behind. Who were these people? What did they need to get away from? Who was that out in the boat, watching them? Why did Blackbeard get so angry? He sure seemed mad, but Logan had only felt unsafe for a moment. Not that he'd needed to. Blackbeard listened to Happy and calmed down. Nothing like his own dad. There was no reasoning with him once he got mad.

Logan stopped in his tracks. When would he stop feeling sorry for himself?

Blackbeard turned and smiled at him, waving him on. Blackbeard, Ma'am and Happy were a lot of fun. No point wasting time wondering who they were. And he could dump the self-pity too. It was time to go climbing.

Out at sea, Oscar and Zach were racing away in the speedboat.

"That was close. No point being spotted and getting them anxious. Last thing we want is them calling the coppers," said Zach.

"That's for sure. We'll hafta take the loot ashore tonight or tomorrow night when they're all asleep. They'd better be gone by Monday or we're gonna hafta give them a load of aggro," Oscar said. "They'll wish they'd never set foot in Hideaway Lodge."

## Chapter Four:
## Rock Climbing

They walked up past the house and along a track amongst the trees. Soon they were standing at the bottom of a cliff about one hundred and forty feet high. Near the top, at about one hundred feet, was the opening to a cave. It looked tricky to climb to—Logan couldn't wait to give it a go.

"It's a big cave," Blackbeard said as he laid out the gear. "What's great about this place is that we can top rope it—there's an anchor set up already at the top of the cliff."

"How are we going to get the rope through the anchor?" asked Logan.

"See that path off to the side about thirty feet up? I'll climb up to the path, and then run up to the top of the cliff. I'll attach the rope to the anchor, then come back and belay for you both."

With that, Blackbeard started climbing up to the path, with no safety gear, taking what seemed to be the trickiest route. He must have done it before, because he didn't pause to work out his next move. He was an expert climber, scaling the cliff easily.

Logan watched Blackbeard's technique as he edged himself up the side. He sure knew how to keep his centre of gravity where he needed it, flagging with his legs. That was a skill his older foster brother, Cole, kept telling him he needed to work on—Logan often ended up swinging out from the cliff like a barn door.

"He's good," then remembering it was Happy he was talking to, added, "He's clamberingly soar-sonic."

"Apingly," said Happy. "But I always feel better when he gets to the top."

She kept her eyes fixed on Blackbeard. Logan saw her body relax when he made it to the path.

"Let's gear up," she said and started putting on her harness.

Logan did the same and by the time Blackbeard had come back down they were ready to go. Blackbeard made them check their gear twice then he checked them both himself.

"Off you go then, Cliffhanger. Don't find the treasure without me," Happy said.

Logan considered his options and mapped out a route in his mind. He was about halfway up when he tried a dyno, a move that required momentum to get to a hold just out of reach. He slapped the hold but didn't latch, lost his footing, and started to fall. Blackbeard locked the belay and Logan hung in mid-air, eighty feet up.

"Good try, Cliffhanger. Not enough push off with your legs!" Blackbeard called out.

"Try again. You can do it!" Happy yelled.

Logan sprawled himself against the cliff, then pushed hard with his leg. This time his hand latched to the hold. Awesome! The other two gave him a cheer. He felt like doing a thumbs up but stopped himself in time. Instead he started moving again, reached the cave and pulled himself in, then detached the rope from his harness and lowered it to the ground. Sitting down near the edge of the entrance, he waited for Happy to arrive.

She chose a much easier route to Logan's, and moved fast. She almost fell a couple of times, but managed to latch a hold. Blackbeard called out several times for her to slow down, but she kept moving like a snake escaping from a fire. She hauled herself over the edge of the cave and clicked the button on her stop watch.

"New record!" she yelled out. Logan helped to untie her,

then lowered the rope down. It wasn't too long before Blackbeard appeared.

He squatted down in front of Happy, frowning. "Well done, Happy, on breaking your record, but I sure hope you're satisfied now. No more record breaking. It's time you worked a little harder on your climbing technique." She nodded and he kissed her forehead, then handed them each a torch from his backpack.

They moved together into the darkness, the light from their torches picking out stalagmites growing up from the floor. In some places they met with the stalactites coming down from the ceiling. Magic.

"Take a look at this," Blackbeard called out. Happy pulled Logan over and they stared at a rock that Blackbeard was holding. In it were some fossilized shells.

"Ammonites," Logan said.

"Ammo at night? That could be painful," Happy said.

"No, dweeb." Logan smiled. "They were animals that were related to octopuses and squid, but they're all extinct now. See their spirally shell? It's made up of chambers, like little rooms. The animal only lived in one of the chambers, and used the other spaces to float. Some ammonites were tiny; others were as big as a person."

"Wow, a geolololo ..." Happy paused. The word combinations were spinning so fast in her head you could hear them banging into each other. She let out a satisfied sigh. "A geo-climb-ologist. Not only climbs them, knows what they're called. I wish you were my brother."

A wave of loneliness surged across her face. It was the same look Poet got when she thought about her parents dying.

He banged his arm against hers. "If you can sing in tune, Steve and Abby will adopt you in a flash. My foster sister has no idea. She tortures every song she sings." He rolled his eyes. "Murder!"

"'Fraid I'll have to keep her then," Blackbeard said. "She sings like her mother. She'll break all the windows in your house." Happy giggled and elbowed him in the ribs. "You are really bad, Blackbeard." She smirked. "I'm so gonna tell on you."

"Don't you dare," he said, and then changed the subject before Logan could ask what was so funny. "How d'ya think these ammonites got up here?"

"That's what's so amazing. Ammonites were sea creatures, so it means that years ago the ocean had to come up this high for them to have been left here."

Blackbeard whistled. "Wow, that's something to

imagine. We're over a hundred feet up! I wonder if there are any more around?"

"Treasure hunt for real!" Happy swung her torch as she took off deeper into the cavern.

They all spread out and started turning over rocks and filling their pockets with ammonite treasures, calling out to each other when they discovered something. After twenty minutes of hunting, Logan had searched the whole cavern.

"Are there any other caves around here?" he asked.

"Janet told me there's a big one in the next cove. It's a bit of a hike over the hill, and it's not so exciting because it's at ground level. No one ever goes there unless they're staying here—this is the only way to get to it," Blackbeard said.

"Unless you kayak there." Happy seemed hopeful. It sure sounded like a good idea.

"Stop looking at me like that, you two. No way. No kayaking, Miss Adventure, until Ma'am says you're ready, or I'll be in big trouble. You know she has a thing about water sports."

Happy put her hands on her hips. Logan flicked his torch at her face. Total pout.

"She has a thing about any sports," Happy said.

Blackbeard squeezed her shoulder. "Come on. That's

not fair. After lunch she promised we'd go down to the racetrack."

"The racetrack?" Logan asked. "Do you mean MacAdden's?"

"Do indeed. We've stayed here three times now and it's mostly because we like to go to MacAdden's and take our car for a spin on his circuit. Do you know it?"

"Yeah. I help out after school teaching junior motocross, so Mr MacAdden lets me race his bike on the motocross track in the weekends." Logan beamed. He loved motocross even more than climbing. He knew his foster parents would find a way to pay for the dirt bike and the gear if he asked, but he didn't feel right about that. Anyhow it didn't matter, thanks to Mr MacAdden.

"Have you ever been on the auto track?" Happy asked.

"Nope, but I love watching. We often come down to see the saloons on a race night. My foster dad and brothers are nuts about them."

Happy and Blackbeard exchanged glances. Blackbeard started to attach a belay device to the rope so they could abseil down.

"Time is getting on. It's almost twelve o'clock," he said. "I'm starving. Let's shimmy on down out of here and see if there's any food back in the house. Janet promised us something tasty for lunch, which is exactly what we need if we plan to pack in some speed this afternoon."

It didn't take long and they were all back at the house, eating a selection of fancy salads, funny little potatoes and baked salmon. It tasted fantastic—like how you'd imagine food in an expensive restaurant would taste.

"I don't know why we can't have a pie done in the microwave." Happy moaned as she pushed the food around her plate.

"Eat it, or you're not going to the track," Ma'am said.

The food was gone in a couple of minutes and Happy was standing by the front door, telling them all to hurry up.

When Logan saw their car his mouth dropped open.

"Is that a Ferrari?"

"Yep. Do you like the colour? I wanted red but Ma'am insisted on boring old blue. I mean if you're going to drive a Ferrari, you may as well stand out don't you think?" Blackbeard said, while everyone got in. Ma'am sat in the back with Happy so Logan could sit in the front. Door-to-door awesome.

Logan stared all around him as they got started. "How come it's got four seats? I thought Ferraris only had two?"

"Nope, the Ferrari FF has four," Happy said from the back.

"You know, the Ferrari Family Fun model," Ma'am said.

"Is that the best you can do?" Blackbeard said, cocking his head and lifting an eyebrow. "There is no way Mr Ferrari is going to go for that. Totally ruin the whole image. Bet it stands for … Ferrari Furiously Fast."

"Nope," Happy said. "Too much like those car movies. Can't you come up with something a little more original?"

Logan rubbed his cheek. "Ferrari Fantastically Fabulous?"

"Good, but not quite enough imagination for me," Happy said.

Ma'am elbowed Happy. "Nothing ever has enough imagination for you."

"I know, Ferrari Fizz-wham Flight-whizzer!" Happy yelled, pushing both arms up into the air. They all cheered.

Ma'am, who'd been Googling on her iPad, interrupted them. "Sorry, Smartypants. It stands for Ferrari Four, after the four seats and four-wheel drive."

"Really?" Blackbeard asked. "That's a little disappointing. Not quite as disappointing as not being allowed to buy the two-seater." He glanced over to Logan, rolled his eyes and complained, "Once again, Ma'am's choice. I wanted the red two-seater. I told Ma'am when we all planned to go places together we could tie Happy to the roof. She was keen, weren't you, Happy?"

Happy sighed. "I'd a loved it."

"Cut it out, you two," Ma'am said. "She would've scratched the paintwork."

Laughing, Logan sat back to enjoy the ride, soaking in the feeling of luxury. He was like soft caramel inside a piece of chocolate, all runny and gooey and surrounded by richness. If only this feeling could last.

At the racetrack, Alex was working on a motorbike while his boss, Mr MacAdden, was finishing his coffee and flicking through some papers on Alex's desk.

"What's this, Alex?" Mr MacAdden asked.

Alex stood up straight. He felt a twitch cross his face so he took a deep breath before speaking. He must stay calm.

"It's a list of stuff for Janet. You know, a stock take of the things she keeps in the basement at the lodge."

"Funny kind of list. What's RY stand for? And what are all these weights down the side?"

"Let's see," said Alex, taking the list from his boss' hands. "It's nothing Boss, just some new fancy stocktaking system she thought she would use. She gave it to me to figure out, but it's all nonsense as far as I can see. I told her to ditch it and count the stuff in her head instead." He dropped the list back upside down on his desk. Hopefully Mr MacAdden would think it meant nothing.

Alex moved to the doorway. "Why's it so quiet?"

"I'm expecting some people. They've hired the track for themselves," said Mr MacAdden, joining him. "They should be here any minute. I'll go down and meet them."

As Alex watched him leave, he relaxed his shoulders, shook his head and let out a long breath. He went over to the desk, took his tally list, folded it and put it away in the bottom drawer. It would be safe there until Monday, when the buckets would arrive, ready for him to count, weigh and load.

## Chapter Five:
## Speedball Hairtrigger

***Saturday Afternoon***

The racetrack was only a few miles away. Shame. The Ferrari ride was over almost before it started.

Mr MacAdden was waiting for them. He looked surprised when Logan got out of the car.

"Logan! What are you doing here?"

Oh no! The last thing Logan wanted was for Mr MacAdden to find out he had been trespassing.

Blackbeard put his hand out for Mr MacAdden to shake. "I invited him to join us for the day."

Phew. Logan felt the heat go out of his face.

Happy pointed at each of them in turn. "We're all pirates today—I'm Happy, Logan is Cliffhanger, Mum is Ma'am and Dad is Blackbeard. No real names allowed."

Mr MacAdden looked at Blackbeard. "You've got to be kidding me. Blackbeard! You don't even have a moustache!"

"He's unco-nerdo!" Happy and Logan synchronised.

Blackbeard shook his head. "They mean incognito."

"I'll remember that one next time I see one of your crew," Mr MacAdden said.

"Maybe you could keep that one to yourself. Otherwise I'm sure my crew would adopt it as my nickname."

Logan frowned. Who was Blackbeard's crew? Maybe Blackbeard was a coastguard too, like Steve. Mind you, there was no way Steve would ever own a Ferrari.

"Are we here to race, or are we here to stand around jabbering?" Ma'am asked. "Blackbeard, how about you take the kids for a spin then we have a go?"

In no time at all, Logan and Happy were back in the Ferrari and Blackbeard had them out on the track, this time with helmets on. Happy was in the front, clutching the dashboard, while Logan sat in the back. Ma'am watched from the sidelines, chatting to Mr MacAdden.

"Let's warm her up a bit, shall we?" Blackbeard said. Then they were off zooming around the track.

Logan held onto his seat. What a thrill! They raced full throttle towards a wall at the end of the track then at the last second slid around the corner! Logan yelled out—that was mouth-gapingly cool! They really were fizz-wham flight-whizzing!!

Happy was yelling, "Faster, faster!" but Blackbeard kept the speed to 150 miles per hour. He stopped and let Logan have a turn sitting in the front, which was even more spectacular. It was something else to see the track race past in a blur as they sped along! When they pulled over both he and Happy let out shouts of excitement.

"My turn now," Ma'am said. "You guys stay over there, and watch me fly!" She jumped into the driver's seat with Blackbeard beside her and sped off. After watching her race a few laps Logan wondered how fast she was going.

"There are three speeds: kid speed, mum speed and idiot speed," said Happy. "Kid speed is 150, mum speed is 165 and idiot speed is 180 up. I can't wait to do idiot speed," she said.

"You are dangerous, Captain Happy," Logan said. "No wonder your dad has to keep an eye on you all the time." Happy beamed and jabbed him in the arm.

After Ma'am finished her turn Blackbeard headed out again by himself and rocketed around the track, taking the corners quicker and quicker with each lap. Finally he started to slow down and came in. He jumped out of the car, whooping in delight. They all cheered.

Logan looked around for the first time. No one was about—no customers that was—and only a few staff. He called out to Mr MacAdden and asked where everyone was. Mr MacAdden glanced over Logan's shoulder, maybe at Blackbeard? He frowned, and then he looked away for a moment. When he spoke he didn't look directly at Logan.

"Some big money's coming with his mates. Asked if he could have the place to himself from lunchtime and paid a ridiculous amount. Then he called and said he wouldn't be here till this evening so I let Ja ... Blackbeard come in, but he'll need to be gone by five."

Looked like Mr MacAdden was hiding something. Usually the place was humming on a Saturday afternoon. There again, there were times when the rich guys came and booked the place out.

They would come from London, a group of them with their fast cars and support crew in trucks, race each other for a couple of hours, then spend the evening down at the local pub. Often they'd go over to France the next day and race there. What a life!

Mind you, there could be benefits for him and Happy too.

Logan jumped down from the railing. "I guess that means we've got the motocross track to ourselves. Shame to let it, you know, dry up because nobody's flinging any dirt around."

Mr MacAdden laughed, and nodded in agreement.

"Come on Happy, let's have a go." Logan started moving off towards the bike shed, but she stood still, her mother's hand pressing down on her shoulder.

"My Mum says she wouldn't trust me on a bike as far as she could throw me." She looked at the ground, her shoulders slumped.

Ma'am looked stern as. She was going to need some convincing.

"Your mum's right you know," Logan said.

"What d'ya mean? I'd be throtta-lific!" Happy looked like she wanted to stomp her foot, the way she stood there with her hands on her hips. Exactly like Poet in a mood. Girls! Can't handle the truth.

Logan shook his head. "You are a ... a speedball hairtrigger—all fast, no smarts."

Ma'am and Blackbeard chuckled and Ma'am relaxed a bit. Happy looked betrayed—her eyes slit like a snake, her face pouted.

"That's not fair. I gotta bril-licious brain! You don't even know me."

"I might not know your name, but I got your number, Captain Happy. Let me see: climbing a rock face at high speed without any safety gear, in direct contravention of the rules," he mimicked Blackbeard's voice, and then continued in his own when he saw a glimmer of a smile. "Racing up a cliffside, with safety gear on this time, but at maximum speed, not caring if you fell and banged yourself hard against the rock." The smile was tugging at the corners of her mouth, so he took a risk and kept going. Maybe Happy could handle the truth after all.

"Screaming 'faster, faster' to your dad when you're already going 150 miles an hour, oblivious to the fact that you could, well, die a fiery torturous death if you crash and burn. All this in less than one day when you're on a nice holiday weekend, supposedly enjoying the peace and quiet. It's obvious you define speedball hairtrigger."

Better keep going before she stopped smiling and launched a counter-attack.

"Luckily for you though, according to Mr MacAdden, I am the best instructor he has ever had for speed monsters such as yourself. Isn't that right?"

Mr MacAdden nodded. "Yep."

"I suggest we start on the minis, after you have had a safety lesson and passed the safety test, of course." Logan looked at Ma'am and Blackbeard. Would they agree? Come on, live a little!

He had Blackbeard on his side, no problem. Ma'am was another matter, but after a minute or two of Blackbeard's persuasion, she let Happy go with him.

As they walked away, Happy whispered, "How did you swing that? I've been begging all year."

"Simple, knucklehead. To get your way with any adult, first make sure they believe you agree with them. Then go in for the kill." He gave her his, 'I know everything about life' look. She giggled and started skipping around him as they walked, asking him all about the minis.

When they got to the shed, Alex the mechanic, an overall-clad man in his early twenties, seemed to recognise Happy. He didn't look too pleased to see her.

"I thought no one was coming to Hideaway Lodge this weekend," he said. He paused, then changed his tone, as if he had realised his rudeness. "Janet was going to do a spring clean. She asked me to help tomorrow. She hasn't let me know she doesn't need me."

"We decided to come late Thursday night. Mum got some time off. We'll be staying until next Thursday. How do you know Janet?" Happy asked.

"I'm her younger brother, Alex." He gave her a forced-looking smile, holding out his hand to shake. Now he sounded friendly—almost. "I help her out when I'm not working here as mechanic. What can I do for you and Logan?"

In no time at all Logan was teaching Happy how to ride the minibike Alex had given her. Once she got the hang of it, she had a blast racing around the juniors track. Logan left her to it and had a turn on the seniors track with the motocross bike he usually rode. It was great having the track to himself. He throttled the bike, thrashing all the jumps. Happy would say it was spine-tingling exhib-err-bering.

He pulled a few tricks, starting with a nac nac then a superman, and finishing with a whip. A noise from the side of the track caught his attention. Everyone was cheering, giving him the thumbs up. Embarrassing! Thankfully no one could see his red face because of his helmet. He rode over to them.

Blackbeard thumped him on the back. "You're the next Louis Vaccaro," he said.

Logan couldn't have smiled any wider—Louis Vaccaro was his motocross hero!

Happy was grinning and asked when she was going to get a lesson on a real dirt bike.

Ma'am looked like a mother bear who'd lost her cub.

Mr MacAdden rescued them all by looking at his watch.

"Is that the time? Sorry, but you guys better head out before the next lot arrive."

It didn't seem to take long to get the bikes and gear away. They were all back in the car and did a couple of final laps of the track together, then headed back to Hideaway Lodge. What a wicked day!

Logan slumped back into the seat of the Ferrari and closed his eyes. He would have to go to his foster family's house soon, back to real life. Hopefully he could keep Happy and her family as friends, not just as a nice memory. They seemed to care for him. If it turned out he would never see them again, he was going to miss them.

Alex put through a call on the work phone. "We got a problem, Boss. The rich guys staying at the lodge are here until Thursday. Somehow we've got to make sure they're out of the way on Monday."

## Chapter Six:
## Truths Revealed

Logan wished he could stay in the Ferrari, even though they were parked in the garage, going nowhere.

"Come on inside, let's have something to eat. I texted Janet from the track, so afternoon tea should be waiting for us," Ma'am said.

Food might not be as fun as the Ferrari, but Logan's stomach seemed keen on the idea.

Inside there were enough treats for it to be like a party. Logan dug in, then started a food fight with Happy. He flicked some pistachios in Ma'am's hair and that was the end of the food fight. Rats.

Afterwards they sat on the couches in the lounge overlooking the beach, feeling sleepy. Well, Logan sat. Happy hung upside down from the beam that ran across the room.

"Steve texted, he should be here soon. He's going to pick up Abby from the train station then come straight over," Logan said as he put his phone back in his pocket.

"How many are in your foster family, Cliffhanger?" Happy asked.

"Six, counting me and my foster parents," Logan said.

"Six, wow. You'd have to tie two of them to the roof of the Ferrari," Happy said. "So tell us who they are and what they're like and what colour toothbrushes they have. Details, please.

Logan smiled at Happy. "You're just like Poet, only sillier."

Ma'am lay on the couch, resting her head in Blackbeard's lap, who was fingering her long hair. "Who's Poet?" she asked.

"She's my foster sister. She's eleven, like Happy. Her real name is Lauren, but everyone calls her Poet."

"Why's that?" The question came from above the beam now as Happy had swung over and was doing the splits on top of it.

"It's a bit of a story. You have to tell me your name first. Fair's fair. You know I'm called Logan, after all."

Happy sighed and her mouth drooped. "I guess so. My boring name is Dominica, but I get called Meeka," she said as she swung upside down again. "I prefer almost anything else though. I like making up names."

Whoa, Dominica! He hadn't heard that name for years. It was like being stabbed in the heart and kicked in the guts, both at the same time! Thankfully she went by Meeka. He could live with that. Logan noticed Blackbeard staring at him, a question in his eyes. Logan forced his face to relax into a smile.

"It's a great name. I like it," Ma'am said. "Let's switch back to calling you Meeka instead of Happy. We'll switch Cliffhanger back to Logan as well."

Meeka's mouth drooped even lower. "I guess so, if you have to. I wish I'd been called Poet. That's ace-ingly superb. Your turn. Tell us the story about why she's called Poet."

"All right," he said. "Lauren, or Poet as we call her, and her brother Cole came from York. Their mother died at Poet's birth, when Cole was nearly five. She used to lecture English Literature. So their dad used to have poetry nights to help them remember her. By the time she was five she had already learned a million poems." Shaking his head he added, "Poor kid."

"No way, I think that's awesome!" Ma'am said. "Poor kid to lose her Mum, though. What happened to her dad? And how come they're living with you guys down here in the south of England. Cawsand's a long way from York."

Logan shut his eyes and leaned back. How much should he tell them? Their stories weren't something any of his foster family shared in a hurry. They often made people feel sorry for them, which was something none of them wanted. They didn't need pity; they needed friendship. What if he never saw these guys again?

If he never saw them again it wouldn't matter how much he told them. Let them hear it all. He opened his eyes.

"On Poet's seventh birthday, they all went for a walk in the park after her party, and their dad was knifed by some man and died right there in front of them."

All three of them gasped, but he kept on before they could say anything.

"They had no other family and after a week or two it became clear to Cole that the Social Services were going to split him and Poet up. He was only about twelve, but he had been helping to look after her since she was born, seeing as they had no mother. He was pretty fatherly about her. Still is."

Logan paused for a moment. Wouldn't it have been great to have a big brother like Cole looking after him after his mother died?

Oh. Everyone was staring at him. He sighed and carried on.

"Cole didn't want to be separated from Poet, so they ran away, caught a train south and ended up living in a container at the Plymouth dockyards. He was getting desperate about what to do next when my foster dad, Steve, found them and brought them home for the weekend."

Logan leaned forward and smiled, "Actually, it was Nate who found them. He stumbled across Poet reading a crocodile poem out loud and they ended up having a fist fight. They're always doing that. She wouldn't tell Steve her name, so he called her Poet."

Ma'am frowned. "Who's Nate?"

"Nathaniel Kelly. Nate. He's Steve's son from his first marriage. He's my best friend, too. Oh yeah, and he's my other foster brother, besides Cole."

"Steve's first marriage?" asked Ma'am.

"That's right. Steve's first wife, Nate's mother, died of cancer when Nate was only two. A couple of years later Steve met Abby and they got married. Then Cole and Poet came to stay for the weekend, but it ended up that Steve and Abby wanted to keep them both. They helped them figure out who'd murdered their dad, which is another story, but in the end they caught the bad guy and he got put in prison, and Poet and Cole came to live happily ever after with Abby and Steve."

"Wow, that's quite a saga," Blackbeard said, shaking his head.

"Is it true?" asked Meeka, dropping off the beam and coming over to stand in front of Logan. She put her hands on his shoulders and stared into his eyes. "Don't lie to me, Logan. I want to know if it's really true."

"Yes it is, every bit of it," he said.

She put her face real close, searching his eyes, then stood up straight and gave her verdict. "Yep, it's true; I can't see any bluffing in there. And I know all about bluffing."

"Ain't that the truth," Blackbeard said.

"So, how old are you all?" Ma'am asked.

"Nate and Poet are both born in June, but he's one year older than her. So, Poet is eleven like Meeka, but she'll be twelve in a month. Nate is twelve now, almost thirteen, and Cole's sixteen, almost seventeen. His birthday's in August," said Logan.

"And you're twelve, too?" Ma'am asked.

"I turned thirteen last month, at the end of April. Nate won't be thirteen for another month, so I'm a couple of months older than him."

"I see," Blackbeard said, "a few months makes a big difference. I bet you're a lot more mature."

Was he joking? Of course not. A few months does make a big difference.

"So when did you come to stay with Abby and Steve?" asked Meeka, who was now squeezed on the couch, lying in front of her Mum.

"A year and a half ago."

Ma'am nudged Meeka then they both sat up. She smiled at Logan and leaned forward. "What about your mother? Is she still alive?"

"Nope, she died, too. Eaten by a tiger," Logan said. That was one topic he didn't need to talk about today.

"That's not funny Logan. Tell us the truth," Meeka said. Logan stared at her. Why was she asking? Couldn't she see he didn't want to go into it?

"I don't think he wants to talk about it," Ma'am said. Thank goodness Ma'am was clued up! He did not want to cry again. Not now. Not here.

He leaned back into the couch. He felt like hugging his legs and hiding his face in his knees. Maybe he *was* ready to go home.

Funny, he had never called his foster family's house 'home' before.

"Let's drop it—we have enough to think about anyway. Imagine that, Meeka. All those kids in one family," Ma'am said.

"And all those parents dying," Meeka said. "Your family makes me feel like I'm normal for a change."

"What d'ya mean, Meeka? Why would you not feel normal?" Logan asked, leaning forward again. It was definitely time to talk about Meeka, rather than himself. All these different emotions were making him anxious, like a worm in a bait box.

"Phew, saved by the bell," Meeka said as the doorbell rang. She turned to Ma'am and begged her, "Please, can you go into the other room, please?"

Ma'am frowned but got up, "Not for long, Meeka. Five minutes max. You've just got to deal with it." She walked down the hallway, away from the front door.

What the heck! Meeka had asked her mother to leave the room, and she had done it!

"That's not nice, Dominica!" Blackbeard said, leaning over her, hands on her shoulders. Better to ask about Meeka and her Mum later. Anyway, right now all he wanted was to see his foster parents.

Blackbeard went to the door and let them in.

Abby came straight over to Logan and hugged him. "It's so good to see you. I sure missed you while I was in London."

Abby's hug felt good, even though it was in front of everyone. Logan clung tighter. How could he not have seen it before? If it wasn't for Abby and Steve; he, Cole, and Poet would have had nowhere to go. They would have been on their own. Worse, he would still be with his father. Who cared if they had actually wanted him or not? He was just grateful they'd taken him in.

He tried to stop it, but it was too late. He sobbed. Like a baby. What an idiot!

"What's wrong with my boy?" Steve asked Blackbeard. Logan could make out anger in his voice.

That was weird—it took a lot to make Steve mad. Logan turned his head to look in Steve and Blackbeard's direction.

"What have you done to my son?" Steve asked, stepping closer to Blackbeard.

"Nothing, nothing, honest," said Blackbeard. "He's been telling us about your family and I think he's a little bit overwhelmed." He stared at Logan, then grinned.

"You have no idea what you just said, do you?" Blackbeard asked Steve, facing him again.

"What?" asked Steve, his eyebrows scrunched together.

"I'll tell you what you didn't say," and taking Steve by the shoulders, Blackbeard turned him so he was looking at Logan, who couldn't keep the smile off his face. "You didn't say, 'What's wrong with my foster child, the one I have to put up with because no one else wants him?'"

Steve paused, as if thinking about what Blackbeard was saying. How would he respond? Logan held his breath.

"Of course not. I love Logan as much as I love Nate and Cole and Poet. I've always thought of him as my son. I've always wanted him in my family," and he stepped over to Logan and hugged him hard. All the traces of the black cloud were smooshed out of his body.

Meeka had moved over to lean against Blackbeard. "We'd better get a towel to wipe up that monstrous swamp of tears on the floor before something starts growing in there."

"Mum would love to see this. She would be balling her eyes out," Blackbeard said.

"Why did you send her out of the room?" Logan asked, wiping his tears on Steve's shirt.

"Don't you dare blow your nose on that," Steve warned, still holding him tight. Logan reached out and grabbed a nearby tissue.

"Come on, Meeka. What's up with you and your Mum?" Logan asked.

Meeka turned and buried her head in Blackbeard's shirt. "You say."

"I think it'd be better coming from you." Blackbeard waited. Silence. He added, "Meeka here has had a few bad experiences lately with friend's parents when they meet her Mum." He then spoke down to the top of Meeka's head. "But if you don't let them meet her, they might think she's a thief, or an assassin, or a … a … "

"Dentist," Logan said, with a shudder.

Meeka looked up, a smile creeping over her face. "I can't have you think that!" She called out, "Mum, you can come back in."

Ma'am walked in and spoke to Meeka, "About time too, young lady. Do you have any idea how hard that was, having to listen to the soppy bits through the door?" She smiled and reached out her hand to Abby. "Nice to meet you, I'm …"

"Lia Castaneda," Abby said, her face in shock. "The singer."

## Chapter Seven:
## No More Play Pirates


Wow! How could he not have known? What a dummy. Lia Castenada! She was mega-famous.

Imagine that. He had stolen the last pancake from her plate, drenched her with the hose, and thrown pistachios in her hair. What about when he had joked that she should give him the Ferrari because she was way too old for a car like that?

Would he be allowed to keep treating her like he had all day? Maybe he would have to start behaving now.

It was kind of sad she was so famous.

"I think you mean superstar," Steve was saying as he shook Lia's hand. "Pleased to meet you. Abby here deals with showbiz people all day long in the fitting room. She judges them not by their reputation but by the amount of work they create for her."

"No special treatment for popularity?" Lia smiled.

"The more famous they are, the lower they go on her popularity scale," Logan said. Maybe Lia would still laugh at his wisecracks. "You're so famous she probably won't like you at all." Abby turned red as she thumped Logan on the shoulder.

Lia laughed. "Maybe if I don't work with her we might get along as, you know, normal people."

That sounded good. Normal must be way easier than famous.

"Do you cheat at monopoly?" asked Abby. Maybe she was trying to find some common ground.

"Never," said Lia, then frowning at Blackbeard added, "Cheats make me mad."

He looked down at his hands.

Abby smiled. "Well then, I might like you after all."

Lia turned to Meeka. "See, no problem."

"Just wait …" she grumped, gloom in her eyes.

"What for?" Steve asked.

"Everything to change. When people find out who my Mum is, suddenly I'm not Meeka anymore. I'm Lia Castaneda's daughter and I must be treated carefully. Everyone has to watch what they say and do around me. And I have to be good and proper all the time …"

"That'd be impossible!" Logan snorted.

Meeka poked her tongue out at him, and then kept talking.

"… or what I do might get published in some stupid magazine. Last time I made a friend at the playground, her Mum fainted when she met my Mum."

Blackbeard rolled his eyes. "You can imagine what Meeka said about that."

Logan winked at Meeka. "Gee, Mum, you need to shower more often."

"Exactly!" Blackbeard laughed before Steve or Abby had a chance to tell Logan off.

Lia was shaking her head. "That is precisely what she said. Can you read her mind?"

"It's a pretty simple mind. There's a lot of space voyaging going on in there," Logan said. Meeka poked her tongue out at him again, and then grinned.

He grinned back then looked at Blackbeard. "Hang on a minute—if Ma'am is Lia Castaneda, that means you're her husband, Jason Whitley, the famous stunt director!"

Blackbeard nodded his agreement. He was Jason Whitley. That was it—no more Blackbeard from now on. Jason Whitley was epic! And real. And standing right there in front of him, in person.

Jason's eyes glowed as he looked at Logan and said, "Did you hear that Lia? He said famous. I sure like this kid. Logan, I'm nowhere near famous."

"You are to me. I think you're amazing!"

"You're not going to faint are you?" Meeka asked, her brows furrowed.

Logan stood there shaking his head, speechless.

"Logan, Mum's famous. Dad's, well … I don't know. Have you seen some of the stuff he does? He's stupid."

Jason laughed. "You know Meeka, I think he believes my stunts are better than your mother's singing."

"Of course!" said Logan, then went red in the face. "Oops. Sorry Ms Castaneda."

"No, it's good to know where you stand right from the beginning." Lia looked at Jason and he nodded. "I think Logan, you can call me Lia. It'd be great if we all got to spend a bit more time together while we're here. We've loved having you with us for the day, and if your foster family are as much fun as you, we'd be keen to meet them."

She smiled at Logan, and then her face became serious again. "Only thing is, you all need to promise not to talk to anyone about the stuff we do when we're together. Even with your friends as school. Chitchat has a way of getting twisted around and passed from person to person until it finds its way to some magazine publisher. Then it creates a whole lot of unnecessary problems. Do you think you can all manage that?"

"There are lots of things we don't talk about with anyone," Logan said. "All that stuff I told you about my family, I haven't told anyone else."

Steve grabbed Abby's hand and squeezed it. Was it because he used the word family instead of foster family? That *was* kind of new. It felt good.

Abby spoke up. "I don't know what you've done today, but you've made a big impact on Logan, and that means more to us than the fact that you're a superstar and you're a famous stunt director. For that reason alone we'd love to spend some time with you, and if it means we have to have some kind of code of silence, I'm sure we can all handle that."

"Poet might need bribing," Steve said.

"No, she's good at secrets," said Logan. Uh-oh, big mistake.

"Oh, what secrets are those?" asked Steve, his eyes glinting.

"Now, they wouldn't be secrets if he told you, would they?" Meeka said. "I think you should go and get everyone and come back for dinner."

She was a master of distraction. Would it work?

Abby frowned and ran her hand through her hair. "No, we couldn't do that. There's too many of us to cook for."

"Oh, we don't cook," Meeka said.

"I have a moral objection to cooking," Lia said.

"And we have a moral objection to eating her cooking," Meeka said without hesitating. Jason smiled.

"Are you going to let her get away with that?" Lia looked at him, folded her arms, and clenched her fists.

"Well," he paused only long enough to put his hand on his heart, "I'm with her on that one."

"Oh, you are, are you? I guess you'll be with her tonight in a tent on the back lawn," Lia said.

"Yes, yes, yes!" Meeka shouted, dancing around them both, "Can Logan and Poet and Nate and Cole and their dog and their cat and their crocodile come too? Please, please, please …"

"Now look what you've done!" said Jason. "Stop it, Meeka. Your mother was kidding. Let's sort out dinner first, eh?"

He turned his attention to Abby and Steve. "We'd love for you to come to dinner, and we'd like to meet Poet, Nate and Cole, though I think you can leave the cat, the dog and the crocodile for another day."

He reached out and put his hand on Meeka's head. "Don't worry about how we'll feed you—if Janet can't get something for us we'll spit-roast Happy here."

Steve looked at Meeka. "You might prefer the crocodile spit-roasted. Happy might not go round us all."

"Oh, there's always enough Happy in this house for everyone," Lia said.

Meeka jumped up and down. "Especially if the kids can go camping!"

Jason looked a little sad. "Sorry, we have no tents."

"We do!" said Logan. "We love camping, and it would be off the grid awesome on your lawn. We could go right down real close to the sand. It'd be like a holiday on a deserted island."

"Or like a holiday on the back of a gimungus sea turtle floating on the surface of the great deep where no one has ever been before." Meeka danced around in excitement.

Steve frowned. "Or like a bunch of kids putting tent peg holes in an immaculate lawn that looks like it's never been walked on."

"Thank you," Lia said. "Someone with common sense. You need to spend some time with Jason. Maybe you could teach him something."

"Common sense never invented the light bulb," said Jason.

"Or tried to fly," said Logan.

"Or land on the moon," said Meeka as she stood beside Jason, his arm around her shoulders. They sure made a good team.

"I could just ask Janet about the tenting," Jason said, a hopeful look on his face.

Logan and Meeka both shouted as Lia punched Jason in the arm. "You're such a pushover," she said.

"Aw, come on, it'd be fun. We could have a fire on the beach and roast marshmallows and sing camp songs and tell scary stories. You could still sleep in your bed. Promise." He looked at Lia with big puppy-dog eyes. She shook her head and smiled.

"Okay, I guess it does sound like fun. As long as Janet is all right with it, and Abby and I don't have to do any work. We'll sit inside and eat chocolate and cake while you guys set everything up. Agreed?"

"Deal. That is, if Steve and Abby don't mind?" Jason asked. "Come bedtime you're welcome to tent or sleep inside or go back to your own home and abandon us to the back of the giant deserted turtle island."

"Sounds like fun. We'll be in." Steve said.

Jason phoned Janet, who was fine about the tenting. She also said she would sort something out for dinner and have it to them in an hour.

Logan went with Steve and Abby to get the others and help with the gear. When they got home, everyone listened to Logan as he downloaded all he could in twenty minutes. The kids didn't believe that he was telling the truth about spending the day with Lia Castaneda, but once Abby confirmed it they yelped and hollered.

Logan leaned against the doorframe and watched them all. He looked over to Abby, who seemed glad to be home as she sat, watching everyone dance around. Her thick dark brown hair was cut short into a bob, and pushed back, as usual, with a colourful scarf. Her African heritage gave her dark skin as well as dark eyes which Logan knew never missed a thing. This should be reassuring, but more often than not, it was just plain annoying.

Cole was swinging Poet around while she attempted to sing one of Lia's songs, completely off-key. Cole and Poet were obviously related, with their blond hair and sky blue eyes. Cole looked pretty strong as he dropped Poet onto the couch. Must be from all the training he did. Mind you, Poet was short and skinny as a weed—with her long blond hair flinging around her face she looked like a dandelion puffball on a stalk.

Nate started tickling Poet. He was like Steve, his Dad, black hair and dark blue eyes the colour of denim. People often asked if Logan and Nate were twins because they were so close in age. Weird. They looked completely different. Nate was average height and solid like a tree trunk, whereas he was taller and skinnier, with dark brown eyes and light brown hair bleached blond by the sun.

Abby smiled at Logan. "How do you think the Castenada-Whitleys are going to cope with all of us?"

He shrugged, grinning. Poet started dancing around the table and singing another one of Lia's songs, off-key again. Cole threw a cushion at her.

Nate covered his ears. "Poet, whatever you do, please don't sing."

On a salvage boat out at sea, the Captain was shouting at Oscar and waving his arms about.

"You've got to get those buckets into the house and off this ship tonight! The coastguard issued me with an inspection notice today. They'll be here tomorrow or the next day, and I don't want to risk them finding anything onboard. Tomorrow night the wind's going to pick up, and you won't want to be anywhere near the water in your runabout. You can't go during the day with people staying there. You've got to go later tonight while they're all sleeping."

Oscar, frowned, wiped his mouth with the back of his hand as he put down his beer, then let out an angry moan. "Okay, okay, let's get loaded up then. Come on Zach." He kicked Zach's feet out of the way as he stalked past him.

## Chapter Eight:
## Fire Stories

*Saturday Evening*

After another classy meal provided by Janet, everyone had a lot of fun setting up the tents. Abby and Lia sat in the house talking about shows and costumes, and every time Logan had to go and get something he found them laughing. They were really hitting it off.

Jason called out to them. "Everything's ready. Come on ladies, let's sit around the fire and tell stories. Hope you saved us some chocolate."

It was Jason and Steve who did most of the talking, swapping stunt stories with coastguard rescue stories. It seemed that Jason liked to throw people off cliffs, while Steve liked to rescue them from cliffs. The makings of a great friendship for sure.

"Sit still," Cole told Nate. He was drawing everyone in turn in his sketch pad. It was a nice change to see Cole relaxing and enjoying himself. Abby said Cole had grown up pretty quick, what with helping to look after Poet since she was born, and then seeing his father murdered. He was always worrying about Poet and wanting to keep her safe. In fact, he was protective about Nate as well. More like over-protective. He was always wary of strangers, but for once he seemed happy to enjoy Jason, Lia and Meeka, no questions asked.

Logan stood up and went to take a look at the sketch of himself that Cole had already drawn. Not too bad.

Cole smiled at him. "I reckon I've never seen you look happier, Logan."

It was true. Wouldn't it be great if this night lasted forever?

It didn't get dark until about nine-thirty, so it was ten o'clock before they started roasting the marshmallows. Logan had hardly left Steve's side all night, Nate was leaning on Abby, and Poet was resting her head on Cole's shoulder, as she often did when she was tired.

Meeka was snuggling up close to her mum. Jason sat on Meeka's other side. It was all very cosy and everyone was enjoying themselves and the marshmallows, although Meeka refused to roast her own. She didn't seem to want to get close to the fire, even though it had died right down.

"Why don't you have a go, Meeka?" asked Nate. "It's fun."

Typical Nate. He found most things in life fun, and if they weren't, he knew how to turn them into fun.

"I'm scared of the fire," she said.

Jason squeezed her shoulder and she moved to lean against him.

"When Meeka was five, I got home after being away for a few weeks," Jason said. "I spent some time with her first then left her with her nanny while I went to surprise Lia, who was in the studio downstairs. The nanny was hopeless. She got talking on the phone and left Meeka to herself. Meeka thought she would cook me some lunch and slapped half a loaf of bread on the element and turned it on full, thinking she would make me some toast."

He paused, stroked Meeka's hair, took a deep breath, and continued.

"The sprinkler system wasn't working—the electrician was coming in the next day to fix it. The tea towel had been left on the stove element and it caught on fire, then the flames jumped onto the net curtains. After that, the room caught fire and there was nothing to stop it. Thankfully the fire alarm went off, but the stupid nanny thought Meeka was outside and ran out looking for her."

He looked stressed, like he might cry. Lia rubbed the back of his neck.

"I ran into the kitchen, and it was all smoke and flames. I got down on my hands and knees and there was Meeka, hiding under her play table. She was unconscious from the smoke. I pulled her outside and resuscitated her. The rest of it … it's a bit of a blur."

"That's because he was so wound up. We all were," Lia said. "He wouldn't leave Meeka's side. He had this terrible burn on his shoulder from reaching under the hot table, but he didn't even notice it. When one of the male nurses at the hospital tried to get him to leave Meeka so he could tend to his shoulder, Jason almost punched him. I had to come up to him and jab a sedative into his arm."

She put her arm around Jason's shoulders and kissed the side of his head.

Jason smiled at her then turned to look at them all. "Hence, Meeka doesn't cook either, although she has mastered the toaster and the electric jug, and she makes a mean peanut butter sandwich. A fine accomplishment I say, and all that is necessary for now."

"I'm still scared of fires though." Meeka gave a sad smile.

Poet sat up straight and leaned towards Meeka. "Don't worry. I'm scared of going to the park by myself."

Now everyone looked sad, remembering Cole and Poet's dad getting stabbed in the park. If only Meeka would transform back to Captain Happy again.

Nate broke the mood. "And I'm scared of sharing a room with Logan, especially after he's eaten baked beans. I sleep with a gas mask under my pillow."

Everyone laughed as Logan jumped on Nate, pushed him to the sand, and started a wrestling match. It didn't take long before Nate had Logan pinned to the ground.

"Unfair advantage!" Poet yelled, and launched herself on Nate's back, causing the tussle to start again. Meeka joined in and between them they overcame Nate, but it took a while and they only managed because Nate couldn't stop laughing.

"Wow, he's got skills!" Lia said, eyebrows raised.

"He's going for his Taekwondo black belt this year," said Steve. "Been doing it since he was five. We can't keep him away from the training centre. He teaches a junior class and does Capoeira and Brazilian ju-jitsu as well. Poet's half way to a black belt, but she prefers dancing and gymnastics. Logan only started a year ago, so it'll take a while for him to catch up, especially as his dirt bike seems to have more priority."

He put his arm around Logan's shoulders as Logan sat down next to him again.

"I can't handle the sparring in Taekwondo. Reminds me of my dad too much. I have to leave the dojang whenever they start that," Logan said.

Steve squeezed his shoulder and Jason smiled at him, understanding his eyes. That was nice, but he didn't want to dwell on it so he gave a big smile back to Jason and said, "I like watching Nate and Cole though. They're really good."

Poet jumped up and did some turning kicks and knife hand strikes into the air accompanied by ninja-like sound effects. "Nate's so quick he could disarm someone with a gun, but Cole's so fast he could deflect the bullet."

Everyone laughed.

"Nate is pretty fast, but there's no way I'm going to be beaten by a twelve-year-old," Cole said. "I got my black belt a couple of years ago. I'll be going for my second dan later in November."

"Awesome, a family of ninjas!" Meeka said. "I tried Taekwondo when I was five, but there was a bully in my class who broke my arm. Now we have someone come in to teach me martial arts at home twice a week. I don't do gradings because I've had so many different kinds of teachers from all sorts of martial arts over the years."

"That's brilliant!" said Nate. "What's your favourite?"

"Well ..." She looked up at the sky. "I loved what Nick Mileson taught me."

Everyone stopped moving and stared at her. Nick Mileson! She'd been taught by the world's number one stunt fighter!

Nate went crazy. "Nick Mileson! You've been taught by Nick Mileson! That's the best! You are so lucky!"

He would have kept going but Jason coughed and gave Meeka one of his organ-burning stares.

She grinned at him and then turned to Nate. "Did you know Nate, that if you spell gullible slowly it sounds like orange?"

"Huh?" Nate mumbled, still lost in the idea of being taught by Nick Mileson. "G... u...l...l...aw, you were pulling my leg about Nick Mileson."

Logan grinned at Meeka. "Was any of it true? Do you know some martial arts? Don't make me come over there and check your eyes for bluffing."

"Everything else was true, Logan. I wouldn't lie to you. Nate, on the other hand, is going to provide me with hours of fun."

# Chapter Nine:
# Smuggler's Frustration

### *Sunday Morning — Early*

Logan convinced Nate to sleep under the stars. The girls shared a tent with Abby. It turned out that Lia was mid-tour and needed to be back on the road again in a few days, so Jason insisted she sleep inside and get a good night's rest. He crashed on the sand next to Steve and Cole.

About one o'clock in the morning, Logan felt Nate shaking him awake. "Bad dream, buddy," Nate spoke in a quiet voice as they sat up in their sleeping bags. "You haven't had one of those for a while. Must be the cold. Was it about your dad?"

Logan shivered. "No. There was a fire. Meeka and I were tied up and couldn't escape."

"Wow, that's the first nightmare about someone other than your father since you moved in. I have to say I'm offended. I thought it would be about me."

"I don't need to be dreaming to have a nightmare about you. I get a fright every time I look at you."

Nate laughed. "Uh-oh, looks like we've got company."

Out from the tent squeezed Poet, still in her sleeping bag. She stumbled over and plonked herself between them, making them move apart to give her room.

"You didn't have one of *your* nightmares, did you?" Nate asked her. Poet often had bad dreams about the night her father was stabbed, even after almost five years.

"Nope, but Logan's moaning woke me up. I thought I might have a bad dream if I went back to sleep, so I came out here instead to cheer you guys up." She swivelled around and lay down, with her head on Nate's lap and her legs draped over Logan's knees. She was asleep in less than a minute.

"Can you believe it? That sure helped a lot, didn't it? Are you feeling cheered up yet, Logan?" Nate asked.

"Nope, can't say that did much for me," Logan said.

"It should, you know. I always feel kind of comforted when Poet does her sleeping on her brother's trick."

"Yeah, why's that?"

"Cos it's good to know that if I flunk out at school I'll be able to get a job as a sofa."

"Right, good point. I'll remember that next time I fail a maths test. What I want to know though is why she always puts her head on your legs and leaves me with her knobbly knees and smelly feet?"

"That's easy. It's because I'm so good looking. Nobody wants to stare up at your ugly mug when they're falling asleep, but one look at handsome me and she knows she's bound to have good dreams."

Logan raised his eyebrows and replied in a polite tone. "I have to disagree, Nate repugnant-face. Personally I think you're extremely ugly, much uglier than me."

Nate stared at him and replied in the same tone, "Actually, Logan loathsome-looks, you are incredibly ugly. You are so ugly that the only friendship you'll ever have is in the pigsty."

"That might be so, but at least my friends speak. The pineapple you keep in your room for a friend is never going to make a sound."

"Would you two cut it out!" Poet growled, sat up and turned to face the ocean. Steve, Jason and Cole yelled out as well.

"I agree," Meeka said, coming out of the tent in her sleeping bag and sitting between Poet and Logan. Abby also called out from her tent, telling them to keep quiet.

Wicked. They'd managed to wake everyone up! Logan and Nate grinned at each other.

"Okay, okay. We'll be quiet," Logan said.

They all sat staring out to sea. Five minutes later Poet and Meeka were about to nod off, when Logan noticed something.

"Do you see that light out there?"

"Looks like it's coming towards us. Must be a boat. Should be close enough to hear it soon," Nate said.

Sure enough, a minute or so later they picked up the sound of an outboard motor. Steve, Cole and Jason sat up and stared out to sea as well.

"Must be someone doing some late-night fishing," Steve said.

"It better not be the paparazzi," Jason said, and stood up. "You guys didn't telephone anyone when you went home, did you?"

"Of course not," Steve said as he stood up.

Jason folded his arms. "I sure hope not."

"Don't be stupid!" Cole said. "Dad avoids the press. They always want to run stories about what a hero he is every time he saves someone's life. He always fobs them off and lets someone else have the glory."

"Abby and I believe in living quiet lives, Jason." Steve spoke calmly. That was something Logan liked about Steve—he always kept his cool, even when he was angry. Cole stood up and Abby came out from the tent and stood beside Steve, holding his hand as he continued.

"We don't need our kids to have any attention from the likes of the press. It'd create a whole lot of stress if anyone published their stories."

Meeka went over to Jason and he put his arm around her shoulders. "Okay, I'm sorry Steve," he said. "I believe you. The thing is, the media are making a huge thing about Lia's tour, even more than normal. It's like her whole life is on show right now. So I'm a little uptight about her having somewhere to go where she won't be hounded by the press. I'm sorry for jumping to conclusions."

Steve spoke, his voice firm. "We do appreciate you taking the risk to let us spend some time with you, Jason. We've enjoyed getting to know you all. But if you want us to leave, we'll go right now."

Logan's heart sank. Surely not? Not now. Not in the middle of the night.

"No, I don't want that. I'd like it if we got to know each other even better. But I need to tell you something," Jason said, shifting about on his feet. "After we had coffee the other day, I had you all checked out by a private investigator."

Logan heard Steve and Abby both draw in a breath of surprise.

"Everything he came back with reassured Lia and me that we wanted to meet you all. According to him, you're one trustworthy family, so I was pleased to see Logan come down the cliff this morning. I was hoping we'd get a chance to meet again." He held out his hand for Steve to shake, which he did after a brief pause.

They turned their attention to the boat and everyone was quiet for a few minutes. What would they say next? Hopefully they could drop the aggro.

The lights on the boat went out, and the motor stopped. Logan stared hard and made out the silhouette of the boat as someone rowed it.

"Why would they turn off their lights and motor?" Meeka asked.

"Might be in trouble," Steve said. He stared a bit longer. "Nope, looks like they're still moving. Wonder where they're headed? I thought they were coming in here but it doesn't look like it now."

They could hear the sound of oars splashing in the water.

"Blackbeard, oh, I mean, Jason, said there was another cove over the hill. Maybe they're headed that way," Logan said.

"Could be," Jason said.

"Smuggler's Cove is what they call it down at headquarters—isn't that right, Dad?" Cole asked. He volunteered with the coastguard when he could, and had even been out on a few cliff rescues.

"Been awhile since any smuggling was done here, but back in the 1700's it was the main source of income for the farmers and fishermen around these parts," Steve said.

"What were they smuggling?" Meeka asked, her eyes cutting across to Steve.

"Tea and alcohol. The government of the day had imposed such hefty levies on tea and alcohol to raise money to pay for its wars that by the end of the 1700's it was estimated that over half the tea drunk in England was smuggled in."

Cole spoke in a hushed whisper. "So, what would happen, was that smugglers would bring over tea from France in the dead of the night, rowing their boats into small coves all along the coast. They'd hide the tea in caves, and wait for daylight. But they would have to ..." and here his voice changed to a shout ... "Watch out!"

Everyone jumped.

"Cole!" Poet growled. "What did they have to watch out for?"

"The ever vigilant coastguard, who'd spot them and shoot them dead. Those were the good ol' days." He sighed, a content smile on his face.

Steve spoke up. "Actually Cole, the ever-vigilant coastguard didn't stand a chance against the smugglers. They mostly had free rein around these parts because nearly everyone in the villages was involved, either in landing the goods, or selling the stuff. You see, it was against the law to smuggle tea and alcohol in, but it wasn't against the law to sell it. So the smugglers would leave the stuff in a cave for someone else to pick up later and they would sell it, never committing a crime."

"Maybe the people in that boat are smugglers, bringing in bad stuff. We should go capture them!" Meeka said, taking a few steps towards the ocean.

Jason reached out and put his hands on her shoulders, stopping her. "Maybe we should go to sleep. It's almost two o'clock."

"Meeka," Steve said. "The people in that boat are likely on a camping holiday, moving from cove to cove. They're probably coming in after fishing all night, and turned off their motor and lights off so they didn't disturb anyone. Otherwise they could be had up for trespassing. Isn't that right, Logan?"

Everyone laughed while Logan squirmed. "I think we should get some sleep. I'm going into the tent."

"Me too," said Poet, and took Meeka's arm. "Come on Meeka, let's get some shut-eye."

Out in the boat, Oscar and Zach rowed to the nearby cove. Only when they were sure they were out of earshot did they speak.

"Tenting on the beach! You've got to be kidding! What kind of deep pockets do that?" said Zach, shaking his head.

Oscar shrugged. "Looks like we got past them though. We'll hafta move this last lot to the house through the tunnel, seen as we can't go up the main beach anymore."

"You know, I'd rather try the beach and risk being spotted by a bunch of mindless money-spinning superstars than have that tunnel collapse on me. Didn't you see it last time? It's going to cave in any day now." Zach shuddered like a fly bouncing into a spider web.

"Cut it out, Zach. Let's land this load and take it to the basement speedy-like, while they're all still crashed out on the beach. The tunnel's all good. If it ain't caved in after all this time, it ain't gonna cave in now."

# Chapter Ten:
## Secret Tunnels and Old Coins

### *Sunday Morning*

Early in the morning, Logan heard Meeka come into the boys' tent and whisper to Jason that she was going into the house to sleep with her mum. He checked his watch—five-thirty—and went straight back to sleep.

He was woken by Nate throwing a towel at him from outside and telling him everyone else was up. When he managed to get himself outside, Jason walked over to him, tagged him on the arm and took off, yelling, "Race ya to the house, sleepyhead!"

Jason was fast, and reached the doorway to the house in front of Logan. He stopped, turned around and gestured for Logan to slow down and be quiet. As Logan approached, Jason put his arm around his shoulders and whispered, "See why I'm one of the luckiest men in the world?"

Inside, Lia and Meeka were singing and dancing to a song on the stereo. They sounded amazing. Meeka could sing exactly like her mother.

"Wow, they sound like angels," Logan said.

Jason smiled. "Yes, they do."

Logan watched some more then smiled wickedly. "Too bad Meeka doesn't act like an angel!"

Jason laughed out loud, and Lia and Meeka stopped dancing and looked their way. Jason stepped inside and gave Lia a hug as the others came up to the door.

"How'd you sleep?" he asked her.

"Pretty good, apart from some nightmares about tigers banging around in the basement. One time when I woke up I thought someone might be down there, but then I figured it was a bad dream, so I went back to sleep. That is, until somebody woke me up by kneeing me in the back." Lia grinned then messed up Meeka's hair.

"I thought I told you to stay on your side of the bed," Jason said to Meeka.

"I did!" she said. "But Mum was on my side of the bed too, and it was bit of a tight squeeze."

Before Jason could respond she added, "I've got one of your favourite songs for you," and she pointed the remote at the stereo and started singing along to the chorus of "Perhaps, Perhaps, Perhaps" with Doris Day. The others came up to the door and listened too. She sang a few bars then flicked off the song and hugged Jason, looking up at him with big pleading eyes. "Please say yes..."

"Wow, that is begging as an art form," Abby said. She turned to her kids, "Don't you ever try that on me."

They all sniggered. They wouldn't dare.

Lia laughed. "It only ever works on Jason—he's such a big softie."

Logan remembered Jason's comment at the door about being the luckiest man in the world. Lia was right—he was definitely a pushover.

"What is it you want, Meeka?" Jason asked, standing up tall and looking down his nose. Sure, like Meeka didn't have him wrapped around her little finger.

"To go exploring over the hill and see if there are any smugglers there, hiding in the cave. Mum said if Cole would go along to supervise it might be okay."

"Whoa, what's this about smugglers? You never mentioned anything about smugglers," Lia said.

It took a few minutes, but Jason filled in Lia on the events of the night. Her disapproval of Meeka's scheme was written all over her face.

"Dad could come with us, and then we'd be fine," Meeka said.

"Nope. We made a deal, buddy," Lia said. "Yesterday

you had your dad for adventuring. Today I've got him for relaxing. We're going to sit around and enjoy the sun, maybe go swimming and chillax. We haven't seen each other for a month."

That sucked. They'd never get another chance to see the cave in the other cove if they didn't go today!

Logan looked around and caught Cole watching him.

"You know, Dad," Cole said to Steve, "we could call through to Sam at headquarters and ask him to swing by the cove on his way out to sea to check if whoever was there last night has moved on. If it's all clear, then I could go with the kids to explore. Like you said, it was probably just someone tenting for the night. There are no smugglers around here these days."

Cole was on their side. It might work yet!

"That's right, Dad," Nate said. "Plus Mum's been away all week, so you'd be able to have some time to yourselves without us lot bothering you before you have to head out with the volunteers this afternoon for rescue practice. We'd take the walkie-talkies so we could contact you if we needed to," Nate said.

How could Steve turn them down now?

"I don't know," Steve said. "It is a good idea to have Sam check though. No one is supposed to camp there. It's private property."

"Why don't you phone him, and we'll think about it over breakfast," Jason said. Meeka winked at Logan. It was going to work out. They'd be going to the cove for sure.

Logan loved the breakfast as much as the dinner the night before. Janet turned up with primo food—freshly cooked muffins and pancakes, then bacon and eggs that she cooked on the spot for them all.

"Sorry for spoiling your spring clean," Meeka said to her after breakfast.

"What spring clean?" Janet asked.

"Your brother, Alex, told us at the track yesterday that you wanted him to help with a spring clean here today," Meeka said.

Janet frowned. "I didn't have a spring clean planned. Mind you, Alex often gets things mixed up. He has a lot going on in his mind. I'll give him a call later and set him straight."

Meeka walked away with Logan, "That was strange, huh? Wonder why Alex thought Janet wanted him here."

"Yeah, I've never known anyone to get upset about missing out on spring cleaning," Logan said.

"And this place is so cleantubulous it doesn't need any springing!"

Logan stared straight at her and raised his eyebrows. "I wouldn't know. Nobody's offered to show me around."

"Come on guys!" Meeka called to the others. "I'll give you the tour while the adults decide our fate. Everybody show them your pit-sad-aful eyes." The adults laughed as the kids left the room, with their eyes wide open and hands begging.

The house was over-the-top luxurious. Poet, who was known to speak furniture, stood in the middle of the formal lounge, gaping.

"Wow, those couches are so snooty, I can't understand a word they're saying," she said.

Meeka laughed. "Nah, they're just pretending." She went over and jumped up and down on one of them. Poet covered her eyes and squealed until Meeka hopped off.

"Take a look at all these old books," said Cole, running his hand over a row of books in a huge bookcase. "You guys keep going. I'm going to stay here for a while."

They left him to the bookcase while they explored the second floor, which held countless large bedrooms, many with their own fireplaces and bathrooms. Every room oozed elegance. Maximum cringe.

Nate elbowed Logan. "Look at Poet. She's in a daze."

"She's going to be rearranging her bedroom for weeks," said Logan.

"I don't get why she's so blown away by it. It's just furniture."

"Yeah, and you can't even stand on any of it."

"Exactly. Every piece of furniture is screaming, "No Foot Zone". My feet are in agony."

"Torture," said Logan.

Meeka called out from the doorway. "Let's go down to the basement."

She led them down some stairs. Cole joined them again at the bottom.

"There's an underground tunnel behind this door that leads to one of those locked doors in the boat house. Janet told me about it, but she said it's kept locked at both ends because it's so old now that it's not safe. I'd love to go down it," Meeka said.

"Sweet, a secret tunnel. Maybe it leads to the local pub as well. That's how the smugglers would get down to the beach in the middle of the night," Nate said.

"Bet there is a couple of skeletons lying in there from when the smugglers had a fight and shot each other," Logan said.

Poet grimaced and wiggled her fingers in front of her face. "With big rats and spiders crawling all over them."

"Gross." Meeka smiled. "Can anyone pick a lock?"

"Cole can," Poet said.

Cole shook his head. "No way, guys. If it's locked, it's locked for a reason. I'm not going to have to tell Lia Castaneda that her daughter got squished flat as a pancake under a pile of falling rocks. Don't think she would sing very sweetly about that."

Everyone moaned.

"Hope I don't get as boring as you when I'm nearly seventeen," Nate said.

"You can be thankful I am boring. I heard the adults talking, and they all think I'm a nice responsible young man. You know what that means don't you?"

"We can go to the cave!" Meeka shouted.

"Sounds like it." Cole looked across the hall. "What's behind this other door?"

He turned the handle but it wouldn't open.

"More storage for food and stuff Janet uses for the guests. She doesn't want little rats like me getting into the chips and cakes," Meeka said.

Poet got down on her hands and knees. "There's something stuck under the door. Looks like a coin or something metal." She pulled out her pocket knife and flicked out the object with the back of its blade. It was an old-fashioned coin.

Cole studied it. "I think I saw a book upstairs about coins like this. Do you mind if I take it and check it out, Meeka? You guys could find out if we can go to the cave and get ready."

"Sure thing. Last one up the stairs has to carry the most stuff!" Meeka raced ahead to the front living room where the adults were sitting, drinking coffee and talking. The others followed in slow mode, nervous about knocking anything over. They heard Meeka squeal and knew they were going to the cave.

## Chapter Eleven:
## Plans Are Made

It was a steep climb to the top of the cliff, but a great race down the other side to the cove. Logan would have won but Nate kept pulling at him to slow him down. Cheat! Still, it was hard to be mad at someone when your sides were sore from laughing so much.

The sand was warm from the sun—too warm for the waves, which were constantly coming in to try and dance on it, but then recoiling from the heat back to the ocean. As Logan was watching it, Meeka came up to him.

"What you doing Cliffhanger?" she asked.

"I was just thinking how the waves remind me of you," Logan said.

"How's that?"

"They never sit still."

"Exactly. I wanna see the cave—let's go." She tugged on his arm.

The cave's entrance was like a large slit between the rocks—a giant's doorway. Cole told them to turn on their torches as they headed in. Wouldn't it be freaky if someone grabbed them as they stepped inside?

"Watch out for bogey monsters," Poet said.

Logan stepped in behind her.

"Boo!" shouted Nate, from off to the side.

Logan jumped and hit his head on the rock. "Ow! Nate, you idiot!"

"Oops, sorry," Nate grinned. "Come on, let's take a look around."

A cavern opened before them, with shells and pebbles strewn over the sand. It was about thirty feet around. They searched the rock wall, hoping to find an entrance into another cavern. Nothing. They all groaned in disappointment.

Poet lay down on her back in the middle of the cavern, and Meeka joined her. They waved their torches, crisscrossing their beams on the roof, making a light show.

"Did you see that?" Logan called. "Up there!" He was pointing to a gap in the rocks a little over eight feet up. When they looked closer they found handholds that almost looked like they'd been chiselled out of the rock. Logan scrambled up and helped the rest of them through the gap.

Inside was another cavern, as big as the first. It was eerily quiet, with only sand on the ground — there were no scrunching sounds of shells underfoot. In fact, the sand seemed almost groomed, as if someone had raked it—or dragged something heavy over it.

"Look at this, guys." Poet was holding out a coin she had found in the sand. Trust her, her curious eyes never rested. Cole took the coin from the basement out of his pocket. Exact match.

"What did the book from the library at the house say about the coin?" Nate asked.

"Not much. It wasn't the right kind of book." Cole seemed disappointed. And something else too—worried? Cole always suspected the worst. The coins were old, and probably valuable. Didn't mean anything suspicious was going on, though. Or did it?

"We could Google it," Meeka said.

"Or we could Gomander it," said Nate.

The others all laughed, except for Meeka, who was obviously baffled.

Logan helped her out. "He means we could ask our history teacher, Mr Gomander. He collects old coins. He's mind-derailingly boring about them. I bags to wait outside and keep a lookout for smugglers. There's something about

Mr Gomander I don't like, and he doesn't like me either. But might just be my inability to grasp historical concepts."

"You know, concepts like time management." Nate was smirking. "If only you could get your homework in by the due date, you might stand a chance of getting into his good books."

Cole said he would phone Mr Gomander when they got back home and ask to meet him the next morning at his place. There wasn't much else to be discovered in the cave, so they headed outside again. They found the remains of a fire further along the beach, but it looked too old to have been lit the night before.

Nobody else was about, and there were no more caves to explore, so they went for a swim, lay in the sun and played football. Cole acted as rogue, helping whichever side was losing. After playing for an age, everyone sat down to rest and eat chocolate.

Meeka laughed. "This is double rainbow brilliant."

Logan smiled at her, remembering her lonely look from the day before. She must be one sad kid if this was double rainbow brilliant. Apart from inside the cave, they hadn't even climbed anything.

Nate said, "Come on Meeka, you must have heaps of fun living the life of superstar daughter. Friends galore, concerts and parties. Sounds like a dream."

Meeka sighed and leaned against Logan's arm. She looked like she was ready to cry.

"There *are* a lot of concerts. I often go with Mum on tour. But it's a lot of stress for me because I hate the crowds. I could never perform like she does in front of all those people. I can't even sing in front of a roomful of friends. It makes me feel like throwing up. So even though the atmosphere at her concerts is buzzarific, I get nervous for her before every show." She poked the sand with a stick. "As for parties, I am only eleven. I'm not allowed to go to many parties, and the ones I do go to I find pretty boring. I'm not much into them. Probably because I don't know many people."

Yep, he was right. There was a tear or two, splattering the sand.

Logan put his arm round her shoulder like Nate did with Poet when she was upset. He waited for her to get control of herself.

"Surely you have lots of friends? After all, you're so much fun."

The others all murmured their agreement and Meeka looked up and gave a thankful smile as she wiped her eyes.

"Dad's away most of the year at one movie location or

another, and Mum goes on tour at least once a year, then performs all around the UK when she's not on tour. She's home a lot more than Dad, but we miss him so much we try and spend some of our time out on location with him, so I'm homeschooled. I have a tutor and a minder, but not many friends. It's pretty difficult to keep friends when you don't spend much time in one place. Plus there's the whole daughter of a superstar thing. Sometimes I think it's easier to not even bother."

She sighed so hard she could sink a few feet into the sand.

Poet looked like she was sinking into a hole too. "So when you finish your holiday, you'll be going on tour or out with your dad somewhere and we won't get to see you again for ages. If at all."

Poet had really taken to Meeka. They'd been laughing all through breakfast that morning—a couple of giggly girls sharing deep secrets.

Logan had liked that. It was true Poet could be silly, but usually only when she was with Nate. Most other times she was serious and sensible, especially around other kids. It was like her sense of humour had been squashed flat when her father died and now she was mostly quiet and calm, like Steve. It was great to see Meeka bringing out her fun side.

Come to think of it, Meeka was bringing out the fun in him too. If what Poet had said was true, he was sure going to miss Meeka. He had only known her a day and a half, but she had crept under his skin and sneaked into his heart. He was beginning to think of her like a sister, in the same cool way Nate thought about Poet.

Meeka squeezed his hand. "We better make the most of our time then. We're leaving on Thursday, so we've still got a few days of fun left," she said. She was forcing a smile, trying to seem happy. She was probably embarrassed about crying in front of them. She was right though—they should make the most of the days left.

"You know, maybe your parents would let you stay at our place until Thursday," Cole said, "Make it much easier to solve the mystery of these coins, and we could maximise our Meeka moments."

There, Cole had mentioned the coins again. He *was* worried about them.

"Sounds like an infomercial," Nate said. "What d'ya reckon, Meeka? How would you like to experience life at the Kelly-Parker-Seagate household?"

"Huh?" said Meeka.

Nate put his hand on his chest then pointed to the others as he spoke. "You know, firstly and most importantly, Nate

Kelly, then Cole and Poet Parker, and last but not least, Logan Seagate. Ta-da. The well-adjusted Kelly-Parker-Seagate family."

"Oh, you mean the KellSeaPark family," Meeka said. "Or maybe the Parkly-Gate family."

"Definitely not. Kelly comes first."

"We'll have to take a vote later," said Cole, "once we've tried a few more combinations."

"Good idea," said Nate. "In the meantime Meeka, if you come to stay, I can promise you sleepless nights, an annoying sister, brave and handsome brothers, grumpy parents and a chocolate chip cookie competition as an attempt to make up for the hideously boring meals."

"Do you have microwave pies?" Hope lit up Meeka's eyes.

They all nodded.

"I'm in!" She turned and gave Logan a sisterly hug, "Bet you'll be glad to see me go by Thursday."

"If you eat my share of the cookies, I'll be kicking you out way before then," he said.

Mr Gomander put down his phone after talking to Cole later that day and frowned. So, Cole had found some old coins at the beach. What if they were from the lodge? Maybe Cole would bring the people from the lodge with him. That could be helpful. Perhaps he should get some sedative to quiet them down so he could keep them out of the way for a while. Mind you, with all the martial arts Cole and Nate did, he'd likely need more than something in their drinks. Best to have Oscar and Zach nearby in case he needed some help to, err .... *detain* them.

# Chapter Twelve:
## Shipwreck Clues

*Sunday Afternoon*

Back at Hideaway Lodge, Logan leaned against the wall with Nate and Cole, listening to the parents talk. Meeka stood in between them, doing her best begging act. Her parents needed a lot of convincing before they would allow her to stay at Steve and Abby's without a minder.

"What do you think a minder is?" Logan asked Cole.

Cole shrugged. "Must be some kind of babysitter, or nanny."

"Poor kid, that's worse than a big brother watching your every move," Nate said as he elbowed Cole.

Jason seemed the most unsure about Meeka staying over. He was leaving for Spain the following week, and was going to miss her. However, when Meeka reminded him that the private investigator had declared Logan's family to be trustworthy, he had to agree to let her stay. Still, he made the proviso he and Lia would have dinner

113

with them each night. Excellent. It would be wicked to spend some more time with Jason. Oh yeah, and Lia.

Meeka seemed to love their home. It was no superstar mansion, but Logan loved it. It was an old rambling three-storey house just outside of town, set back among the trees. From the top floor you could see the ocean. The house had been done up, but it still looked old. The wooden staircase, doors and framing gave it a comfortable old-fashioned charm.

The back yard was lower than the front yard, so that the ground level was a basement which was used as a music room, sewing room and gym. The main living area was on the first floor, with an entrance from the front driveway and garden, but was one level off the ground at the rear of the house. The next floor had four bedrooms and a bathroom.

Cole and Poet each had their own bedroom, Nate and Logan shared, and Abby and Steve's room was at the end of the hallway. From the road the house looked like it was only two storeys high, but from the back yard you could also see the basement, making the bedrooms three storeys off the ground.

They all stood in Poet's room, looking at the treetops directly in front of them. Meeka whistled.

"Rainfor-ob-ulous! Where are the monkeys?" she asked.

Logan laughed and pulled her into the room he shared with Nate, taking her to the window.

"No way!" Meeka's eyes were as wide as saucers. "I don't believe it. That is incredi-tastic!" She was staring at a gravity-defying tree house, clinging with an iron-fisted grip to the trunk of a tree, at the same level as the bedroom window. It was almost fifty feet up from the ground, set amongst the branches, one of which came close to the house. A high-sided bridge had been built from the tree house, across the branch, to just below the window ledge, and was held in place by some big hooks clamped into the wall.

"Who made this?" Meeka swung around to the boys, who were all smiles.

"Dad did. He's been working on it since I was born. Isn't it cool?" Nate was beaming as he opened the window and climbed out onto the bridge. "We all help now, which is why it never gets finished. Someone's always moaning they want another piece added. Especially Poet. You can't satisfy some people. Wanna come see? Unless you're scared of heights, that is?"

Logan glanced at Meeka and she grinned at him. "Behave yourself, Meeka," he said, hoping she would stick to the bridge and not try find another way across. "It's a long way up, and there's no rope."

"Yes, Sir, Mr Safety. You sound like my dad," she said as she jumped onto the bridge and ran across to the tree house. She roamed around, touching everything, obviously delighted. "Do you sleep out here?" she asked Logan.

"Only when Nate's snoring gets really bad. It's pretty cold out here. Plus the squirrels attack if you disturb them at night."

Meeka stared into the branches as if she was hoping to spot a vicious pulp-pounding squirrel. "So you were serious about the squirrel pounding you to a pulp and storing you for its winter feed."

The others wanted to know what she meant so they explained the whole CHAD thing, making everyone laugh. Everyone, that was, except Steve and Jason, who came up behind them as Logan finished.

Jason looked over the edge of the fence. "What do you think Steve? I have this need to prove we can be reckless. What d'ya say to dangling children by their feet over this here bridge of yours?"

"Sounds like fun. I wonder how loud they'd scream if we bounced them off the branches?"

"Shame, that could be almost enjoyable," Logan said, "but I think I hear Mum calling us in for dinner. You wouldn't want to upset her now, would you, Dad?"

Steve stared at him. He had noticed. That was the first time he had ever used those words. It didn't sound too bad. In fact, it felt kind of … snug.

Jason nudged Steve. "Act normal. Most parents are used to being called Dad and Mum. It's very uncool if you cry now."

"I'm not crying, I had something in my eye." Steve reached out and punched Logan in the arm. "Come on son, let's go eat."

Jason, Lia and Meeka raved about the food. Of course they would. Steve and Abby's paella was legendary, after all.

During dinner, Lia asked what the kids were planning to do the next day. Meeka jabbered away about going on a bus trip to the next village to visit their history teacher.

How could she be so excited?

"You have been on a bus before?" Logan asked her.

"Nope. Never. I get driven everywhere," Meeka said.

"What about the underground? You must have been on that, you live so close to London." She shook her head. No? She must be kidding!

"So you travel all over Europe, yet you've never been on a bus or the underground?" Logan said, looking over to Nate, who was also shaking his head in disbelief.

"Don't worry Jason, Lia." Nate picked up his spoon and waved it in Meeka's direction. "Our classes in Ordinary will sort her out. We will ban chauffeured cars and aeroplanes for the next few days. It'll be strictly foot power, bicycle power, and bus power for you from now on."

"Whoa, hold on there," Logan said. "She may need easing into our Ordinary classes. They can be quite difficult for newbies. I suggest we allow the occasional Ferrari ride if she gets the jitters."

"Escorted, of course, by one of her fine instructors," Nate said.

"Of course, goes without saying." Logan grinned at Jason, who let out a laugh.

"Afraid the Ferrari ride is out boys, at least for tomorrow. I phoned Mr MacAdden this afternoon and he said he had booked out the track to a group of racers from London. They want the whole place for themselves tomorrow afternoon. Can't understand that, can you Logan?" Jason asked.

Weren't the rich guys from London there yesterday?

Mind you, the place was still empty when Jason and Lia left. Of course! It wasn't the London guys who'd rented out the track yesterday after all.

"It was you guys who booked out the track yesterday!" he exclaimed.

Jason nodded. Whoa, that must have cost a packet.

Logan shook his head. "What a lot of fun that was, huh? I can see why the London guys like to have the place to themselves."

"It was good, eh?" Jason said. "Shame the London guys have got the place to themselves tomorrow, but Mr MacAdden felt sorry for us seeing as we can't use it. He said it'll be okay for us to come watch. He also suggested I might like to bring my nephews and nieces. Do you know where I could find a couple of fill-ins?"

"That'll be a bit tricky. I'll have to think about that one." Logan frowned and put two fingers up to his lips.

Cole, Nate and Poet threw their spoons at him.

Jason smiled and suggested they all meet at the track at about two o'clock the next day.

Lia came back to the bus trip topic and asked why the kids wanted to see their history teacher.

Uh-oh. This would worry her.

Meeka showed her the coins they'd found in the house

and the cave and explained that Mr Gomander would be able to date them.

"How do you think this one got in the cave?" Lia asked Cole.

"Can't say, but Mr Gomander might have an idea. He knows who buys coins like these," Cole said.

Lia looked anxious, her forehead creased.

"There'll be some simple explanation," Steve said, gathering up the dirty dishes. He stopped mid-pass of the serving dish, a look of surprise on his face. "You know, there's a boat not far out to sea, doing salvage work. The inspectors are planning on boarding it soon because it looks like it's leaking oil. Maybe the crew have found an old shipwreck loaded with bullion. That would be exciting, huh?"

"What kind of shipwreck would have coins like these?" asked Jason, turning the coin over in his hands.

"Old ones, with coins like that. Probably from the sixteen or seventeen hundreds. Lots of ships went down between England and France back then. When the wreck of the Merchant Royal, which sank in the sixteen hundreds, was recovered a few years ago it had about seventeen tonnes of gold and silver coins on board. They were worth around 250 million pounds."

"Shimmering silver, that's a lotta loot!" Meeka jumped up on her chair and held her hands out wide. "Imagine how many Ferraris that would buy!"

Unbelievable! That kind of money could cause a whole lot of trouble. Especially if someone *was* trying to smuggle those coins.

"Who gets to keep all the money?" asked Poet. "Is it finders' keepers?"

"Not quite," Steve said, smiling. "British law states any salvage within twelve nautical miles of Britain must be registered with the Receiver of Wrecks. After a year, if no owners are found to claim the ship, it belongs to the Crown, though the salvage company will have Salvage Rights."

"What's that?" asked Nate.

"Salvage rights means they get to do the salvage, and the Crown will pay them an amount for what they find. What the Crown pays depends on lots of different factors, like how hard the salvagers had to work to extract the salvage. For older shipwrecks, the salvage company might get eighty percent of the find and hand the rest over to the government. Whatever the case, it can be a long drawn-out process for all involved, especially the salvage company."

"These coins probably aren't from a shipwreck. That seems a bit far-fetched. Maybe a collector was staying at

Hideaway Lodge and got a bit careless," Cole said, glancing at Logan. Looked like Cole didn't want to worry Lia, either.

"Maybe they had the coins in their pocket and went down to the basement to raid Janet's storeroom, and then the ghosts from the secret tunnel next door scared them away so they never realised the coins had fallen out," Meeka said, leaning over, her eyes wide and her hands outstretched.

"That'll be it, for sure," Logan said.

"Except for the ghosts from the secret tunnel, who are looking for the coins even now." Cole sounded downright spooky. The girls screamed and the boys joined in, and started chasing them around the house until they all fell on the couch laughing.

After being awake so much the night before, they all went to bed early that night. Hopefully Meeka wouldn't think Ordinary was equal to Boring, seeing as all they did was play a few card games. Enough laughs to make her almost wet her pants, but not exactly the ideal superstar evening entertainment.

At least Jason and Lia hadn't asked any more questions about the coins.

Logan lay in his bed, listening to Nate's heavy

breathing. What if someone was smuggling coins ashore? Lia did say she thought she had heard someone in the basement during the night. What would anyone want with the basement though? It didn't make any sense. His imagination was getting away with him. Must be Meeka's influence.

# Chapter Thirteen:
# The Songwriter

*Monday Morning*

At five o'clock Logan was disturbed by Poet moaning in her sleep. Poet? What was she doing in their room? Logan peered over the edge of the bed and saw her asleep on her father's beanbag. It was the one her father had sat on with her to read stories, and was one of the few things they'd brought down from Cole and Poet's home in York. When Poet had a nightmare she would often come in and curl up on it, while Nate would tell her jokes to cheer her up.

Poet thought of Nate as her best friend as well as her brother. For once though, wouldn't it be wicked if she thought of him as enough of a brother that she would wake him up for a joke or a story when she was scared?

He sighed and glanced at Nate, asleep on the bunk beneath him. Funny that such an annoying guy could be both Poet's and his best friend. It was probably because they knew Nate would do anything for them—he was always looking out for them.

Logan lay still, listening to the wind in the trees. It would sound kind of scary if you weren't use to it. Especially if you were worried about the ghosts of smugglers. He climbed down from the top bunk and went to check on Meeka.

He stood at her door, peering at her bed. The sheet was pulled up over her head and he heard sniffles.

"Meeka, it's Logan. Are you okay?"

The top of the sheet was yanked down revealing a very wide-eyed Meeka, obviously trying to be brave. The wind was making more than its usual amount of noise. It'd be pretty bad out at sea, it seemed so wild.

"Shove over," Logan sat on the bed next to her and leaned against the wall.

"Thanks for coming, Cliffhanger." She seemed relieved, but trembled when another howl sounded. "I wish Dad was here."

Logan stared at her. What now?

"You know what he would say?" he said, trying to match the smile in his voice to the one on his face.

"What?"

He mimicked Jason's telling-off voice. "Don't be such a girl."

The next thing he knew, she had thrown off the blankets, picked up a notebook and stormed out of the room, slamming the door behind her. He heard her stomping down the stairs and groaned. That didn't go well.

Steve was standing, dumbfounded, in the hallway, his shaver in his hand.

"What happened?" he asked.

"I called her a girl," Logan said.

"I see," Steve's face remained straight, not even a glimmer of a smile appeared. "My advice is ice-cream. Don't worry about Mum's rationing system. I'll explain the situation."

"Thanks. Warn her that I might need a lot." He went to the kitchen and raided the freezer. Meeka had stomped all the way to the basement, and he went down with the ice-cream held in front of him as a peace offering.

Meeka had one hand on her hip, the other jabbed the air with her notebook. "Don't you dare call me a girl. I am not a girl, I'm a ... a ..."

"A pirate?" Logan asked, and held his breath.

"No, that was the other day. Today I'm a songwriter. What flavour is that?" She pointed at the ice-cream.

"Strawberry."

"That'll do I guess. My favouritist is Cookies and Cream."

"I'll remember that next time. If you'll come again, that is. We don't get many songwriters here."

Meeka smiled at him, took the ice-cream, and said, "I guess I could come back if you get Cookies and Cream. Do you want to see my song? It's horrendible. I was mostly trying to take my mind off the ghosts."

Logan sat down at the piano with the notebook. It had printed staffs and she had scribbled in notes and written a chorus and verse, all about friendship. He played it on the piano.

"Did this come out of your head?" he asked. She nodded. Wow!

"You didn't use the piano to help?"

"Nope." She started smashing at her ice-cream with the spoon, making it all soft and runny. "How long have you been playing the piano?" she asked.

"Ages. I taught myself, so I'm not very good. I don't like it much, but my dad had one, and whenever I practiced he would leave me alone, even if he was drunk. One time I played it for three hours straight so he wouldn't start yelling at me."

He stared into space, mangling his face at the memory.

Meeka stopped slurping her ice-cream. He felt her gaze and turned in time to see her sad expression. She was sorry for him. Funny though, it didn't bother him. It was nice to have a friend who understood. Anyhow, she didn't dwell on pity. All she did was squeeze his shoulder then change the subject.

"You're right. You're not very good—I'm much better. But hey, I practice three hours every day."

"No way, three hours a day!" What was his dad compared to that? Imagine how awful it would be practising three hours every day! Surely that must count as child abuse too!

"Yep, I love it. Mum and Dad think it's great because for at least three hours a day they can be pretty sure I'm not getting into any trouble. I've been playing since I was four. Going to be an astounda-mungus concert pianist when I grow up."

She slurped her ice-cream.

"You'll have to get over your stage fright. You can't go throwing up all over a concert piano. It would be a bit messy."

"I can do piano on stage, because you don't have to look at the crowd. I can pretend I'm all alone in a big bubble, just me and my piano and Mum and Dad." Meeka waved her spoon in a circle shape as she spoke.

"Hey, you've eaten all the ice-cream! What about me?"

Her hoeing through that huge plate of ice-cream was more unbelievable than the fact that she practiced piano three hours a day.

"Oops, here you can finish it," and she handed him the nearly empty plate. "What do you think my name should be, seeing as I'm a songwriter today?"

Logan thought about it as he finished off the ice-cream. "How about Lyric? You and Poet would kind of match then."

"That is double-barrel mind-blastingly brilliant, Logan. I love it!"

Logan listened to the rhythmic thud, thud, thud as Meeka jumped on and off the seat in the bus shelter. Did she ever stand still? He climbed on the top of the rubbish bin and pulled himself up onto the shelter's roof. Meeka followed and sat next to him, swinging her legs over the edge.

"Guys, you're not allowed up there. Can't you read?" Cole said, pointing to the sign.

"I have a moral objection to reading," Logan said.

Meeka grinned and bumped her shoulder against his.

Logan bumped her back. "Anyhow, this is the best spot for playing Notice."

"What's Notice?" Meeka asked.

"It's a game Poet and Cole's dad taught them," Nate said. "You have thirty seconds to look behind you, then you turn around and tell us as much as you can remember. The person who notices the most wins. Cole is the official Notice Champion, but Poet comes a close second. Of course, I've managed to beat her a few times, but Logan is hopeless."

They played Notice until the bus arrived ten minutes later.

"You guys have got elephantine memories!" Meeka said when she lost the last round. "That was thirty things you remembered Cole, and I only got eleven. How did you do that?"

"He secretly is an elephant," said Nate. "That's why he's always putting his nose into our business; it's so long he can't help it."

Cole frowned at Nate. "It's just practice Meeka. You'll get better."

"Well, I'm going to have to practice a lot," she said. "I can't let Nate beat me again."

## Chapter Fourteen:
## Blindly Into Danger

It was less than a three mile bus ride to Mr Gomander's house at the north end of Millbrook. Meeka had fun noticing things about the other people on the bus and whispering to Poet. There was an awful lot of pointing and sniggering going on in their seat. Luckily they were sitting at the back, so none of the passengers realised they were being visually examined and analysed.

Logan was glad of that, because there were two big, tough-looking guys sitting near the front who made him feel uneasy. As a child, men like that visited his father's house and Logan had developed a sixth sense about whether they were good, bad, or wildly random. Something about these two guys was bothering him. A lot.

When they stood to get off the bus at the end of Mr Gomander's street, the men did, too, and they strode off in front of the children. They seemed to pause outside Mr Gomander's place, but then kept walking. Must be his imagination again—surely Mr Gomander would never have anything to do with men like that?

Mr Gomander met them at the door. Meeka smiled at Logan and raised an eyebrow. She probably thought Mr Gomander looked like a friendly old granddad, with his thinning hair, fat stomach and twinkling eyes. But their gleam faded when they saw Logan.

"My my, Logan Seagate. Can't keep away from your favourite teacher, eh? You better behave. I can still issue detentions during holidays." Logan's eyebrows pulled together, and Mr Gomander told him to relax before he turned his attention to Meeka.

He held out his hand for her to shake. "Who have we here, a new student?"

"My name is Lyric. I'm staying with Logan and his family for a few days."

Mr Gomander frowned briefly, but then seemed to remember himself and pulled a smile onto his face.

"Lyric, interesting name. Write songs, do you?" he asked.

Meeka nodded and winked at Logan. One thing about Mr Gomander—his mind wasn't thinning like his hair was.

"Come on in, I can't wait to see the coins you've found," he said.

Mr Gomander lived in a two-storey house on a hill. He showed them the views of the lake from the balcony, before taking them into his lounge. It was a clutter haven, with floor to ceiling shelves crammed with books and papers. A large collection of framed coins hung on one wall.

"Wow, it's a real omnium-gatherum," Meeka whispered to Logan who frowned at her. She rolled her eyes. "You know, a collection of this and that. An omnium-gatherum. Kind of like your family."

Logan shrugged. Where did she come up with these words?

"Morning tea time—thought you might be hungry." Mr Gomander pointed to a jug of juice and a chocolate cake on the table. "Help yourselves."

Cole gave him the coins to examine while he poured himself a drink. The others sat on the edge of their seats, waiting to see what Mr Gomader would say.

Mr Gomander's face went tense and his voice rose. "Where did you say you found these?"

"In the house where my parents are staying, down by the beach," Meeka said.

Mr Gomander put the coins in his lap and focused all his attention on her. There was something close to eagerness in his eyes. "What house is that?"

Meeka's face flushed and she hesitated. Of course, she wasn't supposed to give anything away that might let people figure out who her parents were. But Mr Gomander was so old, there'd not be much chance he would know her mum. Plus, he probably only watched boring documentaries; not the action flicks Jason made.

"They're staying at Hideaway Lodge," Logan said.

Was that a look of satisfaction on Mr Gomander's face, as if he had just ticked something off a list?

Time to change the subject. "What type of coins do you think they are?"

Mr Gomander shook his head as if to clear his thoughts, and then launched into teacher-talk about the coins. "What you have is an extremely rare English Rose Ryal minted between 1604 and 1619. It was issued by King James I, and was worth thirty shillings. It was really a two Ryal coin, but is known simply as the Rose Ryal or Rose Noble. After the Rose Ryal, a coin called the Spur Ryal was minted."

He picked up a pen and wrote down some letters on a piece of paper then showed them. They were what was stamped on the front of the coin and read: IACOBUS DG MAG BRIT FRAN ET HIBER REX. He explained that this translated roughly to 'James by the grace of God King of Great Britain France and Ireland.'

Mr Gomander then wrote down the letters on the back of the coin as well. DNO FACTUM EST ISTUD ET EST MIRAB IN OCULIS NRIS. He explained that they translated to something like, 'This is the Lord's doing and it is marvellous in our eyes.'

"These coins look quite worn, but I'd still consider them to be in good condition. I guess they'd fetch anywhere from fifteen hundred to three thousand pounds each at auction. You should get them valued by an expert," he said.

Everyone stared at him, amazed. Except Meeka, who wasn't fazed at all. Maybe she got that much for pocket money.

"That's meritorious," she said. "Maybe we could do that this afternoon."

Nate shook his head. "We can't today, Lyric. We're busy with your parents all afternoon at Mr Macs, then your parents are coming back to our place before we go into Plymouth for dinner, remember? Maybe tomorrow. You guys are here till Thursday, so we've got time."

A look like relief washed over Mr Gomander's face, and then his expression changed again. Another frown. What was going on with him?

"Sorry Cole. I just realised that juice was a little old. Better not drink anymore."

He stood up and took Cole's half empty glass and the jug of juice out to the kitchen. "I'll get you some more."

Cole looked at Logan with his eyebrows scrunched together. "Strange," he said. "The juice tasted fine."

Mr Gomander came back into the room and handed Cole a fresh glass of juice.

"Who's Mr Mac?" he asked. "Another way of saying McDonald's? Please don't tell me they've opened up down here while I wasn't looking. I think I'd sell up and move to the North Pole."

Mr Gomander seemed innocent enough. But for some reason, Logan was getting his familiar uneasy feeling every time he looked at him.

"No," said Cole, "he means Mr MacAdden's. I doubt Lyric's parents have ever eaten at McDonald's." He looked at Meeka.

She shrugged her shoulders. "Dad does. But we prefer Abby and Steve's cooking. They make great paella."

She turned to Mr Gomander and started waving her arms around. "Have you seen their house? It's rainforest wild—there are trees everywhere. It feels like you're in the Amazon."

"I can imagine Logan swinging from branch to branch," Mr Gomander said. "Explains why he can't sit still in class."

"Maybe if you attached a rope from the ceiling he could hang there like a monkey," Nate said.

Logan felt his face get hot.

"Mr Gomander, do you have a bathroom I could use?" Meeka asked.

Logan figured she was trying to rescue him and he flashed her a grateful smile.

"Down the hall on the left, Lyric. Third door." Mr Gomander pointed, and then asked the others if they wanted some cake.

While she was gone they discussed who the coins could belong to. Mr Gomander wasn't able to shed much light except to suggest that a collector must have left them by mistake. He promised to ask his contacts if they knew of anyone losing some coins.

"Surely if someone lost coins like these at the lodge they'd talk to Janet about it?" Logan asked as they were walking back to the bus stop. For some reason Cole kept yawning.

"If we ask her, she'll want to keep the coins in case someone does talk to her about them," Poet said.

Their faces fell. Those coins were worth a lot of money.

Cole put his arm round Poet. "It'd be the right thing to do."

"Not today though," Meeka said. "No time, we've got to get home then go to Mr MacAdden's. Then we should skip the restaurant with the olds, and you guys should take me out for fish and chips on the beach and a movie as part of my Ordinary training. I heard Nate say Monday night is cheap night at the movies, so it has to be tonight."

Cole snorted. "Since when do you worry about cheap night?"

"Never." She smiled. "I'm practicing being Ordinary. Do I get a gold star yet?"

Mr Gomander watched them leave then sent a text, "All clear."

Next minute there was a knock on his door. Oscar and Zach. Mr Gomander let them in with a scowl.

"What happened? I told you to come an hour ago. I wanted you here before the kids arrived so you could help me with them if I needed to lock them away for a while."

"Sorry, boss, trouble with transport," Oscar said.

"Never mind. As it turns out, luck is on our side. I

thought the girl staying at the lodge was called Meeka, but for some reason she's calling herself Lyric. Took me awhile to figure out she was the same person. Anyhow, she's staying with Cole's family today, so she's out of the way for now. It sounds like they'll all be at MacAdden's this afternoon, even the parents. You'll be able to keep an eye on them there while you start moving the stuff, and then tonight they'll be in Plymouth while you finish the job. Mind you make sure they don't head back to the lodge this afternoon."

Oscar nodded and twisted his fist in the palm of his other hand.

"Take it easy, Oscar," Mr Gomander said. "You better come and go through the back entry so they don't spot you. We should be clear to move the stuff until at least eight-thirty while they're having dinner in Plymouth. Let's get in and out of the lodge quickly and quietly while they're all somewhere else. No one needs to get hurt or even know we were there."

"So no need to rough anyone up? Shame," Zach said, cracking his knuckles.

Oscar smirked. "Come on. Let's get back to the track before the London guys turn up."

## Chapter Fifteen:
## Lost Treasures

*Early Monday Afternoon*

Cole fell asleep on the bus and took a lot of shaking to get him awake. Once they were home he had a cup of coffee and fell asleep on the couch and missed the big ceremony Logan and Nate made of heating up and eating microwave pies. Somehow though he heard them talking about leaving him there to sleep and he dragged himself off the couch and had another cup of coffee. Eventually he was ready to go and they got on their bikes and headed to Mr MacAdden's.

Steve and Abby were at work, so it was just Jason and Lia there to meet them. They all chatted away, smiling and laughing, as they sat on the railing watching four sports cars race around the track. They were throttling it: a Ferrari F12 Berlinetta, a Lamborghini Aventador LP700, a McLaren MP4-12C and a SRT Viper.

Logan sat by Jason who kept giving him information about each car's engine and performance. Jason was a real petrolhead, and Logan soaked up everything he said like a sponge.

After a long time the racers took a break and Logan looked around. He was surprised at the number of support vehicles parked nearby—five big trucks plus a number of smaller ones. Cole joined Jason and Lia and went to talk to the race crews, but Meeka wanted to go take a look at the motocross bikes. The four of them strolled over that way, trying to peer in all the trucks.

"Look at those guys over there," Poet said. "Weren't they on the bus this morning?"

Logan's head snapped round. Poet was right. They were the roughnecks from the bus who'd made him feel uneasy. What were they doing here?

"Guess they drive one of the trucks so they had to take a bus to get around town. Probably visiting some friends and weren't allowed to take the Viper for a spin. Bet that ripped their nightie," Nate said. "They did seem a little grumpy."

Logan's eyes widened. "They weren't grumpy. They were sullen, surly and ..."

"Curmudgeonly," Meeka said. Logan stared at her. Another word! How did she do that?

"Do you read the dictionary for fun?" Nate asked.

"Only at airports. Helps me stay calm. Otherwise I find airports very discombobulating with all those people milling around. One time I caused a mass evacuation with my Nerf gun. I was trying to get a group of people to move away from me by shooting at them."

She raised an imaginary gun and pretended to shoot Nate. An expression of sorrow and regret settled on her face as she dropped her arm and shook her head. "It didn't end well."

Everybody stared at her, mouths dropped. Her expression changed again to one of curiosity as she pointed to the men who were moving away. "We should go see what those nerve-frying tough guys are up to don't you think?" She took off in their direction.

"Uh-oh." Logan looked at Poet and Nate. They all shook their heads and ran off after her.

As they came round the side of a truck, they almost bumped into the men standing at the back of a van that had its doors open. Logan saw a dozen big white buckets with lids on, stacked on top of each other. One of the men pushed the van doors closed.

"What you kids doing back 'ere?" he growled, a fierce look on his face. Nate moved in front of Poet and stood by

Logan, who'd grabbed Meeka's arm and pulled her back.

"We wanted to see if there were any more cars back here. Thought there might be a Bugatti Veyron," Logan said.

The man's face relaxed. "Not at nearly two million pounds a car. Even these guys don't stretch that far." He nodded at all the trucks, then frowned again and snarled at them. "Now scram. We don't want no kids mucking around back here, trying to nick off with stuff."

The kids hurried away, heading for the motocross shed, not talking until they got there and sat down, leaning against the wall.

"He looked as friendly as a wildcat pulled out of the sea by its tail," Meeka said, hands shaped into cat's claws about to strike.

She was right. How would Poet take it? Logan looked her way.

Poet was trying to control her shivers. Poor Poet. She was bound to have nightmares now about the man that had killed her father. That was the problem with her having a photographic memory—she had told him that some images were burned in her mind and she could never escape them. Especially when something like those men jolted them out of the place she had neatly filed them in her brain.

Poet leaned against Nate and Logan heard her whisper 'Blue Days'. That was her code for, "Please be nice to me, because I'm feeling tragic about my dad." Nate put his arm round her and squeezed her shoulders. She took a deep breath and shook herself.

"Did you guys make out the writing near the bottom of the buckets?" she asked.

Nobody had. They wanted to know more.

"I only saw a few numbers like weights, and some letters." Poet shut her eyes. She was probably picturing the buckets in her mind. "One had the letters RS RY and the other SP RY."

"What did Mr Gomander say our coins were called?" Logan asked.

"Don't you ever listen to anything he says? No wonder you flunk history," Nate said. "They're English Rose Ryals."

"Well, this is the first time Mr Gomander has said anything worth remembering," said Logan. "What d'ya reckon, RS RY on the bucket could be for Rose Ryal and SP RY could be for the other coin he mentioned—wasn't it a Spur Ryal? What if those buckets are loaded with coins?"

Everyone was silent for half a minute.

"We've got to try and see what's in those buckets!" Poet said.

She must have forgotten about the men guarding the van. It was true—money did make you lose your head.

Meeka jumped up. "We'll have to be quick. As I came round the corner, I heard the other man say they needed to unload the van speedy like, so they could get back to pick up another load. He said if they didn't pick up the pace they'd be here until midnight. There must be even more buckets somewhere."

Logan frowned. What if the coins were at the lodge? Surely not! It was way too risky to store stuff there. Only one way to find out. He stood up.

"We can't get close to the van with those guys hanging around. But I could follow it on my bike." He nodded at the motocross shed.

"No way—those guys looked dangerous. They'll mow you down and turn you into road kill." Nate jumped up beside him, almost stomping on Poet.

She frowned at both of them. "And what'll we tell Jason and Lia about you zooming off after a van?"

"I'll leave the back way and catch up to them. No problem." Logan knew what he was doing.

"Sounds like a lollapalooza idea to me!" Meeka said. Logan considered her for a moment then pulled the key for his bike out of his pocket. He always kept it there.

"I'm not sure if lollapalooza is a real word or not, but I do know Meeka Happy Lyric that you can't double on the back and come too." He watched her face drop. Better get going before she started arguing.

He turned to Nate. "Don't worry. I'll make sure they don't see me." Nate was shaking his head and followed him into the shed. Logan knew he was going to try and stop him.

Nate didn't need to worry. The bike Logan always used, the one he considered his own even though it belonged to Mr MacAdden, was gone.

Logan stood, dumbfounded. His bike had always been there! Not once had he turned up and not been able to use it. Mr MacAdden kept it for him.

Poet called from outside. "They're leaving!"

Racing outside, they saw the van trundling down the back exit road. It must have unloaded all its buckets and was heading back for more.

Logan kicked the wall of the shed, then slumped down on the ground.

"Cheer up," Nate said, "If those guys had caught you they would have made mincemeat out of you. You wouldn't have stood a chance. The most violent thing you've ever done is peel a potato."

Logan looked up at him, exhaled loudly, and pointed in the direction of the van. "I wouldn't have got caught. I could outpace them on my bike. Where *is* it?"

Who cared about stupid coins? How would he get by without his bike?

They took another look in the shed, but the bike was gone. Surely nobody would have stolen it? They went looking for Mr MacAdden to ask him about it, but he wasn't around. Nobody else in the office could tell them anything about the bike either.

They stood outside. "Come on, Logan, let's not worry anymore about your bike or those nerve-frying tough guys. There's probably a simple explanation for both of them. Mr MacAdden will know where your bike is." Nate pointed to the race track. "Look—the rich guys are racing again and we've yet to see the Viper beat the Aventador, as you said it would. If it doesn't, you owe me your desserts for a week, remember?"

Logan looked at them all watching him. They were worried about him. A smile launched an attack from the inside, laying claim to his face.

"We can't have that. There's no way you're eating my dessert," he said, then he took off towards the cars, beating them all.

Nate was right, they should forget about those guys and the coins—they'd looked right through the lodge the other day. There was nothing there.

The racing was amazing to watch and Logan stopped thinking about his bike. The circuit covered two miles with a couple of straights which the drivers went flat out on, reaching speeds of over 180 mph. These guys were fantastic racers, but any faster and they'd likely lose control on the corners.

"Man, these guys are great!" Lia said as the cars went past them again.

Jason stared at her, his mouth set straight.

She gave him a sly smile. "They sure were handsome too."

"Is that right?" he said, his face pinched.

"Probably don't cheat at monopoly, either," she said, looking thoughtful. Boy, was she a tease. Jason's face was contorted in mock pain. She laughed, putting her arm around his shoulders.

"Don't worry, honey. You're ridiculously annoying, but

I wouldn't trade you in for any of these guys—or their cars." Lia nodded at the track as the cars whizzed past again. "Hmm, I might trade you for the Viper. Do you think those guys would take you?"

"Not once you tell them what he does to fast cars. He likes to rig them so they flip over and over and then he makes them explode." Meeka clapped her hands together as she explained.

"Nothing like seeing a Lamborghini go up in flames," Jason said.

Logan shook his head. "No way! That would be wicked!"

"You should come see some time," Jason said, and then his attention was pulled back to the track as the first of the cars came round again.

Logan's grin widened. Wouldn't it be brilliant if he got invited to see some stunts?

So why was Cole frowning at him?

Mr MacAdden drove up, parked his car and went into the office, which was directly across from the track. Logan got down from the railing to go over and ask him about his missing bike. For some reason Cole followed.

Mr MacAdden didn't know anything about his bike, either, but said he would check it out and let him know. As they left the office, Cole asked Logan to give him a minute and hustled him behind the office.

"Look, Logan," Cole said. "I know Jason and Lia seem genuine. They only knew us five minutes and they were happy to leave Meeka overnight with us. So I'm not saying they don't like you, but you've been so miserable lately, I'd hate you to pin your hopes on Jason inviting you to watch his stunts sometime. When he gets back to his busy life, he's likely to forget us all. Even if he does remember us, that doesn't mean he'll have time for us."

"You never believe anyone!" Logan said, his whole body taut. "They won't forget us."

"Logan, they're from another planet! He blows up Lamborghinis for a job, for crying out loud!" Cole took a deep breath then continued, calmer. "She's a mega-star, and he spends most of his year travelling the world filming movies. They're having a nice holiday right now, pretending to be normal. But when they get back to their everyday lives I bet they hardly have time for each other, let alone a bunch of misfit kids from the south of England. Enjoy them this week, but don't expect too much after they've left. All right?"

Logan stared at Cole, not wanting to admit he might be right. He usually was. Gloom threatened. Not only had he lost his bike, Cole was stomping all over his dream about being good friends with Meeka and her family. He turned and walked back to the cars, staring at the ground, his hands sunk deep in his pockets.

Jason ambled over to the office to talk to Mr MacAdden. When he saw Cole herd Logan behind the shed, he slipped around the other side of the building to listen. He had taken in most of their conversation.

He sighed, thinking about what Cole had said and kicking himself for making the suggestion about Logan coming to see some stunts. Cole was right. Once they got back to their everyday life, he had to fight to make time for Lia and Meeka. How could he possibly find time for anyone else?

He headed around to the entrance of the office. Mr MacAdden had stepped outside and was watching Logan and Cole retreating. He jumped when Jason came round the other corner of the office.

Mr MacAdden nodded at the office door. "I was inside, at the back window, and I heard Cole talking to Logan. Did you hear that, too?"

"Yes, I did," Jason said, grimacing as he ran his hand

through his hair.

"Oh." Mr MacAdden paused. "You know Jason, it used to be that I was the local racing star—and owner of the racetrack—and everyone wanted to be my friend. Then, three years ago, I had an accident racing. I spent three weeks in a coma, then months recovering. All my friends gave up on me, all except Steve and Abby. They visited me every day and rearranged their lives to keep the track going. I would have had to close this whole place down without their help." He swept his arm in wide arc, then dropped it and stared into space. Shaking his head he set his attention on Jason once more.

"They're not very flashy, Steve and Abby. They keep to themselves and focus on their family. But they're some of the most genuine and loyal people anyone could ever know. So when someone comes along and gets the opportunity to be their friend, if I were that person, I wouldn't want to throw the chance away. I'd organise my life to take advantage of their friendship."

He smiled at Jason and went back inside.

Jason headed back to the cars, forgetting what he had come over to talk to Mr MacAdden about.

Back by the track, Nate reminded Logan of his bet. Logan sat by him and watched the cars. Sadly for him, the Viper didn't beat the Aventador, which made it easier to turn down Jason's post-racing offer of dinner at a restaurant. Nate would take great delight in stealing his dessert for sure. Fish and chips and a movie sounded better by far.

# Chapter Sixteen:
## Smuggler's Interrupted

*Monday Late Afternoon*

They rode their bikes back to the house, Logan racing ahead of the others. Once inside he made for the tree house. He needed some space to rearrange his thoughts, but Nate wasn't long in appearing.

"Meeka's worried about you, and Cole told me what he said." Nate sat down next to Logan. "Don't let him get to you. He doesn't know everything."

"He's usually right about things. We don't call him Wise Old Owl for nothing."

"We call him that to annoy him. He's as dumb as you and me. As dumb as you anyway. Come on! You can't tell the future, so stop sulking about it. You're going to spoil all the fun you could have now, plus you'll make Meeka mad."

Nate looked up at the shelf, and then a huge grin detonated his face as he stood up. "And if you're going to make Meeka mad, you should do it for a good reason."

He picked up an egg and carefully rolled it in his hands.

"Powder bombs!" Logan said. "That would be wicked cool!" Maybe all was not lost!

Logan and Nate had taken weeks to make the bombs, if you counted all the attempts that had failed. First, they'd made a hole in each end of the eggs and blown out the insides. Then they'd left them to dry for a few days. The tricky part was funnelling in talcum powder. For an extra sneeze effect they'd mixed in some pepper as well. Lots of the eggs broke at that stage and they had to start again. Once the bombs were full, they'd taped the ends and left them on the shelf in the hut. Abby would ship both boys to the South Pole if she saw powder bombs inside the house.

"After the movie, we'll go down to the beach and attack Poet and Meeka! They'll never know what hit them," Nate said, grinning. "How many do you think we can fit in our jacket pockets without them noticing?"

It turned out they could fit four bombs each. That could do some damage.

The boys went downstairs, carrying their jackets so the pockets were hidden. They tried not to grin too much.

Poet gave them a strange look. Probably she had guessed they were up to something.

Thankfully Meeka groaned just then. "Oh no, I left my wallet at the lodge. Can we bike past and get it on the way?"

"It's in the opposite direction. Don't worry, we'll pay for you," Cole said.

Meeka shook her head. "No, I wanted to pay for you all."

Everyone protested.

"Come on, guys." Meeka put both hands, palms up, in front of her, and shook them hard. "It's easy for me. I have this magic debit card that Mum's accountant keeps loaded with cash. It's got at least three thousand pounds on it, you know, in case I see something important I need to buy."

"Now that I don't comprehend," Cole said.

"I do," said Nate. "It means the super deluxe meal for each of us at the fish and chip shop, plus our own ice cream and popcorn at the movies. No sharing."

"What's a little side trip to the lodge when you put it like that?" Poet said.

"You've got your key?" asked Logan.

"Oh yeah. I'll run upstairs and get it."

Logan shook his head and smiled.

As they approached Hideaway Lodge, Logan remembered his rope was still hanging over the cliff. Actually, it was Cole's rope. Oops.

Cole gave him a ribbing but Meeka was keen to abseil down it, and the others thought it was a good idea too. They yanked up the rope to get hold of the belay that was still attached near the bottom, and then took turns rappelling down. Everyone was in a good mood, even Cole, who stayed at the top of the cliff to untie the rope. He was going to bike around with the rope and anchors to the front door of the lodge and meet them there, then they'd all walk back to the bikes.

Logan remembered losing his running race against Meeka the day they met. Time to redeem himself. Tagging Meeka he took off in front of them all.

"Race ya!" he yelled.

As Logan rounded the corner, he saw something that stopped him dead in his tracks. He dropped down to the ground, and motioned for the others to do the same. There were men prowling around the lodge, acting like they were keeping guard. They looked dangerous.

It must be the coins after all!

They all crouched down behind some rocks while Logan took another look.

"It's the two guys from the racetrack. One of them has a gun," he said.

Poet let out a moan. "What about Cole?" she asked with horror in her eyes.

Cole coasted through the trees and down the driveway on his bike. He came round the corner and spotted a white van parked out the front of the house. What was it doing here? Was there a mix-up with the bookings? The van sure didn't look like the kind of vehicle the usual resident of the lodge would drive. It was a long way off being a Ferrari.

He looked around, his hands twisting on his bike handles. Next thing he scooted behind a tree.

Just in time. Out of the house came a big tattooed guy with a scar on his face. It was the man from on the bus! Except now he was carrying a gun. The man turned and yelled to someone inside to hurry up.

Cole watched as the other man from the bus brought out a large heavy-looking white bucket and loaded it in the van.

"Get a move on, Zach," said the man with the gun.

"Take it easy, Oscar. We're going as fast as we can," Zach said, shooting him an angry glance.

Cole almost let out a groan as he remembered Poet and the kids. He needed to get to them. Going back the way he had come would be too slow—he needed to get past the van and the house and reach them on the beach before they got caught.

Zach went back inside, so Cole took a chance and approached the van as quietly as he could. Oscar was on the opposite side and didn't notice him, but as he drew level with the van, Zach came out of the house and spotted him.

"Well, well, what have we here?" Zach said as he crossed the path towards Cole in a couple of bounds. He pulled back his arm to let loose a punch but Cole blocked it with an inwards kick. Without putting his foot down he retracted his leg and kicked Zach's head. Zach yelled out and staggered back.

Cole leapt forward, grabbed Zach's shoulder, and pulled him down into his knee as it rammed upwards into Zach's stomach. Without stopping, Cole followed through with an elbow strike to the middle of Zach's face, knocking him over. He lay groaning on the ground, cradling his head.

"Stop!" Cole heard Oscar's loud, deep voice behind him, and turned around to find himself staring down the barrel of a gun. "I think you better come with me. Hands on your head where I can see them. " Oscar gestured with the gun for Cole to walk through the house and onto the veranda. It took a Zach a few more minutes to stop moaning, stand up and stagger after them.

## Chapter Seventeen:
## Cave-In

"They've got Cole!" Logan said. Poet paled as she took a look. She turned back around and sat leaning against the rock, eyes closed.

"Looks like Cole had a good go at one of them," Nate said, watching Zach come out of the house cradling his head. "If they didn't have guns, he would have knocked them both out for sure."

Logan strained to hear what the tattooed man with the deep voice was yelling. "They're going to tie him up in the basement. The tattooed guy called the injured one Zach."

Logan sat down beside the girls. Meeka had her arm around Poet. Poet was freaking out, but then she took a deep breath and a calm, determined expression settled on her face. Logan glanced at Nate—he had seen the look on Poet's face, too. There would be no stopping her. She had made up her mind, and when she did that, she always followed through.

"We are not going to let anyone hurt my brother," Poet said. "We have to go get him. If we can untie him, he'll be able to fight his way out. They'll probably only put one guard on him. We can get to the basement through the tunnel you told us about, up there." She nodded off to her side.

Nate and Logan looked at each other.

"We'll have to be careful not to be caught. And the tunnel could collapse," Nate said. Didn't sound like he was worried—he almost seemed excited about the idea.

"The doors will be locked," Logan said.

Meeka coughed. "You know the other day when Cole wouldn't pick the lock for us? I figured I needed to learn how to do that so I YouTubed it on my iPad. I even got some paperclips to keep in my pocket." She pulled out a couple of large paperclips to show them. "I was going to find some pliers and shape them right, but we all got so busy I forgot. There'll be some pliers in the workshop."

They looked at each other and smiled.

"Let's go," Poet said, and she moved off back the way they'd come. The others followed her. Once they were out of sight around the corner, they headed for the trees and picked out a path to the boat shed. Nobody was about—

either the men didn't know about the boat shed or weren't worried about guarding it.

Meeka found some pliers in the workshop and shaped two paperclips into a L-shaped lever, keeping one for a spare. She inserted the other one into the lock and pushed down on it, then poked a second straightened paperclip in the lock. After a few seconds of jiggling, the lock popped open. Poet hugged her and stepped through into a small bricked chamber.

Logan felt a cobweb brush across his face as he stepped into the chamber beside Poet. The only light came from the open door. His eyes adjusted to the dark and he saw there was an entrance to the tunnel on the far wall. Poet headed towards it.

"Hang on, Poet!" Logan pulled her back. "Don't race off yet. I saw some torches here the other day." He pushed her out of the chamber, and spotted the torches on a shelf. They took one each.

Now what? They needed a plan.

"We'll have to be quiet, especially at the other end," Logan said. "When we get there, I'll listen at the door, and I'll hold up my fingers to show you the number of voices I can hear. We'll wait until it goes quiet, then Meeka can pick the lock. Nate should go through first—he's the best fighter, plus he's the most stupid."

Nate grinned at Logan.

"I'll go next," Poet said, her shoulders pulled back and her lips pressed tight together.

She must be kidding! She's too little! Logan opened his mouth to protest but Nate put his hand up, gesturing for him to be quiet.

"Let me," he said to Logan, his eyes angry, his voice calm.

"Poet, I think you may have forgotten for a brief moment that you are in fact the smallest person here. If you want to rush out and meet those guys head on, that's fine. But I suggest we look around for a first aid kit to take with us, or perhaps something we can use as a stretcher to bring you back on."

Meeka and Logan shared a smile while Poet stared at Nate, her hands on her hips. Nate never stopped looking at her, his expression calm and determined. "What's it to be?" he asked.

"Fine, I'll go after Logan with Meeka," she said, dropping her arms but not dropping her attitude.

"Good," Logan said. "But if it doesn't go quiet we come back here and think of something else. If we try to take on guys with guns we'll all need a stretcher. Agreed?"

Logan stared at Poet, who hesitated then sighed and nodded her head.

They stepped through into the chamber, turned on their torches and headed into the tunnel. Shuddersomely eerie. It was wide enough for them to go two by two. Poet forgot her anger at Nate and clutched his hand as she waved her torch around, spotting spiders. There were scuttling sounds as rats ran away.

Logan heard Meeka swallow hard, and whisper to herself, "Ghosts aren't real." She must be remembering her fight with the smugglers' ghosts she'd had in Poet's bedroom.

"Can you hold my hand, I'm scared?" Logan whispered to her.

She shone her torch in his face. "No you're not," she said, and then they heard another rat scamper away. She trembled and grabbed his hand. "You'll be all right. Ghosts aren't real," she said.

Strewn along the path were stones and small rocks that had crumbled from the roof and wall. They had to take their time, picking their way through the tunnel so as to not trip over. The walls were dripping water. About halfway to the house, by Logan's estimation, puddles started appearing on the ground. They rounded a corner and there was a small pool of water right across the path.

"Let's jump it," said Meeka. Logan frowned—that might not be such a good idea. But Meeka was pulling at his hand, so he jumped with her. He kicked at a stone as he landed, sending it jolting against the wall. It seemed as if the wall shook and shivered, then started pelting them with rubble.

"Get back!" Logan called to Nate and Poet, as he pulled Meeka further up the tunnel. A large slab of rock fell down, followed by a whole lot of smaller stones. It only just missed them.

The tunnel was blocked with Logan and Meeka on one side, Nate and Poet on the other.

"Are you guys all right?" Logan shouted at the wall of rocks.

"We're good. How about you?" Nate's muffled voice came back to him.

"We're okay. What's Poet saying?" Logan asked, straining to hear what she was yelling.

"Be quiet, Poet." Logan heard Nate shout.

"Don't worry; she thinks she can morph through the rocks to get to you guys." Nate called out. More noise from Poet. She sounded mad.

"We'll head back to the house and keep a look out. You guys go careful, all right?" Nate yelled.

"You, too. We better stop shouting now, or someone will hear us. See you later." Logan sure hoped he would see them later. Meeka squeezed his hand.

"We better get going," she said. "Before any more rocks come down."

## Chapter Eighteen:
## Sudden Shock

Logan listened at the door. He could make out two voices coming and going. It sounded like they were collecting something from the room across the hall, going upstairs then coming back. Was it coins they were moving?

The first time it went quiet Logan timed how long it took for the voices to return. Four minutes. Not long.

After they heard the men move back up the stairs, Meeka bent down and picked the lock. It was harder than the door at the other end of the tunnel. It took her almost the whole four minutes before she could push the door open. They shut it again, and waited for the men to come and go one more time.

Once the coast was clear, Logan pushed open the door and scooted across the hall, then leaned against the wall next to the open door. Someone was talking inside the room. He peered cautiously around the doorway and saw Zach, standing over Cole, who was tied to a chair. Zach was sporting a bruised face. Nate had been right. Cole had had a good go at him. Cole was sitting side on to Logan. His face was red near his eyes. He must have been hit in the last few minutes. Zach was saying something about giving him a piece of his own medicine. Logan couldn't let Zach do that—he should rush in there and stop him!

How though? Zach was twice his size and probably four times as strong. Logan knew from experience that he was no match for someone Zach's size. The few times he had tried to fight back against his father had proven he would always lose.

He heard the voices approaching again. Aargh! Too late to do anything now. He managed to get back behind the door to the tunnel in the nick of time.

He leaned against the wall with his eyes closed. Anger, fear, frustration—his emotions were all over the place. When he opened his eyes he saw Meeka looking at him, her body tense, her face scrunched up with worry and questions. She would never stay behind the door if he tried to rescue Cole by himself. They'd have to go together and hope for the best.

He scratched out a layout of the room in the dust on the floor. Cole in the centre of the room, with Zach guarding him. Some white buckets stacked on the left wall, and a big pile of something covered by a tarpaulin near the shelving on the right. There was a door on the far wall behind the tarpaulin—it must go outside.

Meeka frowned, scribbled a path on the other side of the door, and drew some stairs and trees. Trust her! Bet her parents banned her from going back there, so of course she had checked it out. Thank goodness.

Maybe she could pick the lock on the outside door and they could escape that way. If only Zach would leave the room.

Meeka started scribbling a plan in the dirt, accompanied by lots of actions. If it had been a game of charades, she would have been the star player. She wanted to run past the doorway and make Zach chase her upstairs, while Logan freed Cole and took him out the back door. She whispered that she knew a couple of good hiding places, and she was fast. She was certain there was no way Zach could catch her.

She might be right, but she might be wrong. What if she did get caught? There had to be another way! But he could hear the men starting to leave. Zach might start hitting Cole again any minute. Meeka's plan was dangerous, but it could work, and it was the only plan they had.

Meeka handed him the paperclips for picking the outside door lock. They heard the men's voices and footsteps retreat up the stairs.

She slipped out the door and closed it so Zach wouldn't notice it when he went past. Logan listened from behind the door, his whole body tense. He heard Meeka call out, "Oh no!" as if she was surprised to see Zach, then her footsteps raced up the stairs. The next moment he heard the sound of the Zach's feet stomping up the stairs as he gave chase, calling out to the others for help.

Logan ran into the room, crouched down behind Cole, and yanked at the rope around his hands. Lucky he was good with knots from all his abseiling. It didn't take long to untie them. He came around the front of Cole and ripped off the tape covering his mouth.

"Ow! That hurt more than the punches," Cole said. "Man, am I glad to see you! Let's get out of here and find Meeka before they do."

He headed for the hallway door.

"This way." Logan grabbed Cole's arm and pulled him to the back door, then pulled out the paperclips from his pocket. He handed them to Cole, who picked the lock in about five seconds flat. As they opened it, they heard the men coming back. Cole shot up the outside stairs, but

Logan headed the other way instead, hiding behind some big rubbish bins he spotted at the end of the path.

"He's getting away," Zach shouted. Logan watched as Zach ran out of the room and chased Cole.

"These kids are nothing but trouble!" Logan heard Oscar say. His heart sank as he made out Meeka's voice.

"Let me go! Let me go!" She sounded mad! Bet she was putting up a fight.

"You deal with her, Jake. I'll help Zach."

"Sure thing. I don't want to take on that other kid anyway. My face might end up like Zach's."

Jake's voice physically jolted Logan, making him clutch at the wall for support. He would never forget that voice.

His father was here.

## Chapter Nineteen: Captured

Poet was so determined to shove the rocks blocking the tunnel out of the way that she didn't even notice more stones falling.

"I've got to get to Cole!" she shouted at Nate.

"You'll kill us both if you don't stop!" Nate shook her shoulders and yanked her away as another large slab came down right where she had been standing.

"Look at that!" Nate jabbed his finger at the fallen rock. "Right now Cole has got more chance of staying alive than either of us! I'm your brother too, remember!"

She stopped still, staring at him, her mouth dropped wide open.

"What?" Nate asked, his face angry.

"Nothing. It feels like something's pounding my head, that's all. You know, like how the ground would pound you if your parachute didn't open."

No way she was going to say she'd just realised Nate was as important to her as Cole. He was more than her best friend. He was her brother, same as Cole.

Nate relaxed and smiled at her. "I'd catch you. Though I might let you drop the last few feet, just for fun."

Poet gave him a half-hearted smile. "We better go," she said, looking at the crumbling walls. They hurried back the way they came until they were safe in the boathouse again.

They decided to scout out what was going on, so they crept down to where the trees bordered the beach. From there they could see the veranda and the side of the house. Nothing was happening—nobody was around.

They crept back through the trees, past the boathouse to where the trees met the edge of the driveway. The white van they'd spotted at the racetrack was parked with its rear doors open towards the house. The two guys from the racetrack kept coming out the front door, carrying heavy-looking white buckets which they stacked in the van. Poet pointed to one of them and said that Logan had called him Zach. Then Zach spoke to the tattooed guy, calling him Oscar.

Oscar acted like the boss, dropping off a load then prowling around checking on things. He even roamed up to the top of the driveway like he was expecting someone else to arrive.

"Idiot," Nate said. "Why haven't we rung Mum and Dad?" They ducked back deeper into the trees and sent Steve a text. Hopefully he would believe them, though he and Abby were having dinner with Jason and Lia in Plymouth, which meant they were at least forty minutes away. Poet told Nate to phone the police, but then they heard something happening back at the van. They needed to go take a look.

A motorbike had turned up—Alex from the racetrack! He was telling Oscar the guys at the track were waiting for their load so they should hurry up. Oscar and Zach headed inside.

"Logan said Alex was all strange and rude about Meeka's family staying here," Nate whispered to Poet. "Alex must've known those buckets of coins were being kept here, and that the racing guys were coming to collect them."

"Mr MacAdden told me they were heading to France after this, to race on some tracks over there. I bet they unload the coins at all different spots around the continent. But where does it all come from?" Poet asked.

"From the sea, of course," Nate said, letting out a deep breath. "It's just like Dad said. Some salvage company has found a huge treasure of old coins which they've been storing at the lodge, waiting for the racing guys to come collect it. They're going to sneak it into Europe so they don't have to declare it."

"Because then they'd have to wait at least a year to convert it to cash ..."

"And they'd have to pay some of it to the government," Nate said, running his hand through his hair.

"Greedy pigs," Poet said. "If they hurt Cole over a bunch of old coins I'll ... I'll ..." She didn't get a chance to come up with a threat because Cole himself sprang up from the stairs at the side of the house. He spotted the van and ran in the opposite direction, down the side of the house towards the beach.

"Get him," Zach yelled as he came up the stairs. Alex jumped off his motorbike and joined in the chase, overtaking Zach. Poet and Nate moved through the trees, trying to keep quiet. Cole ran fast, but Alex was just as fast as he was. If only Cole could get away! But no, Poet saw Alex leap at Cole's back, pushing him to the ground. She started to call out, but Nate clamped his hand over her mouth.

Cole landed on his shoulder and rolled onto his back, then used his momentum to spring to his feet and face the punches Alex was trying to shower on him. Cole dodged them, then grabbed Alex's wrist and twisted it, put him to the ground and stomped on his stomach. Alex lay there groaning, clutching his middle.

"Jerk," Poet whispered. Cole should have knocked him out.

Zach was close behind Alex. He ran straight at Cole and grabbed him by the neck with both his hands, as if to choke him. Cole reacted by kneeing him hard in the groin, causing Zach to yell out, but he didn't let go.

In one fast movement, Cole slammed the palm of his hand into Zach's chin, pushing his head back. Cole then pulled his hand back and rammed his fingertips into Zach's throat. At that Zach let Cole go, and Cole grabbed his shoulders and pushed him aside as he moved past him, ready to run.

"I wouldn't go anywhere," the big tattooed guy said. Oscar. This time he wasn't pointing his gun at Cole, but held it to Poet's head, grasping her by the arm. He let her go to push Nate on ahead of him, and then he grabbed her arm again, so tight it hurt.

She'd let them all down by calling out. It was her fault they were all caught now.

All except Logan.

## Chapter Twenty:
## Disappointment

Logan was leaning over, hands on knees, fighting off a wave of nausea. His father was some kind of criminal, a hired thug at the least! Why was he surprised? When he thought about it, it was the kind of behaviour he would expect from his father. Logan had been deluding himself with his daydreams of a wonderful father, champion of the world in hiding. He wasn't hiding. That father didn't exist.

Logan shook his head and stood up. Now the initial shock was over, he could push it aside and focus on what needed to be done.

Meeka. He had to get Meeka out of there.

Logan crept to the edge of the door, and listened to the struggle Meeka was causing. She sure knew how to kick.

"What you need is a good whack to quieten you down," Jake said.

Logan's blood ran cold and he started to tremble, like he used to do when he knew his father was about to lash out.

But this time his mind reasoned with his emotions. His father wasn't in charge any more. Jake had no right to hit him, and he had no right to hit any of Logan's friends, either. He had to do something even if he did get hurt. And he had to do it now.

Logan stormed through the door and launched himself onto his father's back.

"Don't you hit her. Leave her alone you jerk!"

He threw his arms round his father's neck and tried to yank his head back. Jake grabbed Logan's arms and swung him over his head, throwing him hard onto his back on the floor, winding him. Jake looked like he was ready to punch Logan, then he realised who it was. Shock and some other emotion registered on his face. Was it guilt? Whatever it was, it was gone in a moment.

"Logan!" he shouted, "What are you doing here?"

"What are *you* doing here?" Logan gasped through the pain. His father looked at him with something close to remorse on his face, but then he glanced at Meeka and his expression changed to anger. He grabbed her, and then tied her up. Next Jake tied up Logan, back to back with Meeka.

Logan stared hard-eyed at Jake the whole time, not saying a word. His own father was tying him up. Not exactly the caring father he had dreamed about. It was almost funny. He could have laughed, if only the ropes weren't so tight.

Jake's hands shook as he took out a cigarette, lit it, put it in his mouth, and took a long slow drag. Finally he spoke.

"I only took this job because I was sure you'd be nowhere around. I figured even though you lived pretty close, there was no way you'd ever meet the kind of rich crooks that stay here."

"You're the crook. The family that stay here are the best kind of people. And they're worth a hundred, if not a thousand of you."

Anger flickered in Jake's eyes, and then he sighed and said, "Sorry you feel that way, son. Not that I don't deserve it—I know I do." His shoulders dropped. "I'm not a crook, just so you know. This is the first time I've done anything like this. I got in some trouble and needed some money. It's supposed to be easy money. Nobody said anything about you and your foster family turning up." He paused, looking at Logan.

How did that make a difference? He was still a criminal.

Jake kept going. "We'll be finished soon and we'll be out of here. Someone will find you later, so you'll be okay." He seemed like he was trying to reassure himself. "Sorry I missed your birthday. I guess I'm going to have to go find somewhere quiet to live now you and your foster family have seen us here. I'll be missing most of your birthdays for a few years."

"They're not my foster family. They're my real family. Steve's my father, and Abby's my mother. They'll remember my birthday so don't trouble yourself." Logan felt cold and hard. Jake went and stood outside for a minute. He threw his cigarette away and came inside, rubbing his hands together.

"Right then. Two more loads and we're out of here."

He took a bucket and went upstairs.

"I'm sorry about your father, Logan." Meeka sounded tragic. Logan leaned his head back against hers, glad for her kindness.

"I'm sorry he tied you up. I don't know what I would have done if he had hit you," he whispered to the air.

Meeka laughed. "You were wild-eyed awesome! You looked like some mad bull in a bullring. I almost saw froth coming out your mouth!"

"Gross!" Logan managed a smile.

"Sprayomatic! A little longer and you could have drowned him in saliva."

Meeka's imagination was kicking in again. She was going to be all right. If they waited it out, someone would find them. Surely his father wouldn't let anyone hurt them. Would he?

Jake came back in and took the last load to the inside door. He stopped and came back to lock the outside door again.

"The door to the stairs will be locked too, and I think I'll pull that bookcase in the hall in front of it for good measure," Jake said. "We'll be long gone before anyone finds you. Goodbye, Logan. Sorry I've been such a disappointment to you. Hopefully you'll make a lot better choices with your life than I have with mine."

And then he was gone.

## Chapter Twenty-One:
## Deadly Peril

Cole stared at the gun. If Oscar hurt Poet or Nate, Cole would make him pay.

Oscar forced them all—Cole, Poet and Nate—inside the house, and had Alex tie Cole up while Zach held onto Nate. Oscar kept hold of Poet.

"We'll take these two with us," Oscar said, nodding at Poet and Nate. Anger and frustration ripped through Cole and he strained against the ropes.

"Cut it out, or I'll put a bullet through her foot," Oscar said.

Surely not! He looked like he meant it though. Cole froze. Oscar kept his gun pointing at Poet as he handed her over to Alex, and rung through to someone he called Boss. Obviously Boss was really in charge.

Oscar hung up. "We'll just take the girl. When we're all clear, we'll let her go. Understand? No coppers, or she's a goner. Take her out to the van, Alex, and tie her up."

Alex tugged on Poet's arm, pulling her towards the front door as Jake came up the stairs with the last load. Oscar was studying Nate with an evil look on his face. Jake stared at Oscar, put the buckets down and moved towards him.

"What's up, Oscar?" he asked, his fists clenched tight.

"Don't come any closer Jake. I think girlie should see this, make sure she knows we're serious. And you, fighter boy," he said, nodding at Cole, "You definitely need to know I'm not mucking around."

Oscar pointed his gun at Nate.

"No way, boss," Jake said and lunged at him, knocking the gun from his hands, before landing a blow to Oscar, who clutched his stomach and bent over double.

"No one said anything about killing kids. You can't do that—it's murder," Jake shouted.

Oscar dived forward, grabbed the gun, then turned and shot Jake in the thigh, sending him rolling on the floor in agony.

"This is a serious situation. Don't no one tell me how to handle it." Oscar gasped as he stood up.

Alex twisted his hands together while Zach let out a long slow breath. Cole willed Nate to stay calm. He worked even harder at loosening the ropes tying his hands. Nearly there.

Oscar looked at Alex and Zach. "Right then, let's get moving. Zach, help Jake."

He turned back towards Nate, and then pointed his gun at him.

As the gun pressed on his temple, Nate ducked down and spun to the side, his arms up, knocking Oscar's hand and sending the gun flying. Then he spun the other way, and brought his heel down hard on Oscar's foot while elbowing him in the stomach. Oscar doubled over again, pressing Nate over with him. Nate grabbed Oscar's shirt, and taking advantage of Oscar's loss of balance, he tucked up sideways then yanked Oscar over his shoulder and onto the ground.

Cole managed to twist his hands out of the ropes he'd loosened. He leaped at Zach, ducking a fist in the face before punching him hard in his neck. Zach staggered and fell to his knees.

A shot went off.

Alex had picked up the gun and fired it at the ceiling. He stood off to the side, apart from them all, pointing the gun at Nate.

"Shoot him," Oscar yelled, furious.

## Chapter Twenty-Two:
## Fire Trap

"Meeka, I've got a knife in my jeans' pocket," Logan said. These ropes were too tight to even wiggle his hands about.

"Ewww, I'll have to touch your butt." She sounded horrified.

"Don't be a moron! These ropes hurt. It's worth a try." Meeka poked at his butt and fished out the pocket-knife then tried to cut the ropes.

"This isn't as easy as it looks in the movies," she said.

"Come on, piano girl. Your fingers should be dancing over that knife. Unless, of course, you don't really practice three hours a day," Logan said.

"Jerk."

"You can do better than that. How about ugliojerkio, or fartiofaceio?"

"Shut up. I'm concentrating. Do you want this bladio through your handio?"

"Nopio."

"Didn't think so, you twitiot schnook."

Twitiot Schnook. That was new. What's a schnook?

Meeka was almost finished cutting through the ropes when Logan noticed something moving outside the window.

Flames.

His father's cigarette. It must have caught on the dry grass. He yanked his hands apart, then turned and started untying Meeka.

He turned her to face him before he spoke, trying to keep the alarm out of his voice. "Meeka, you need to stay calm. I'm going to get us out of here."

What would Meeka do when she saw the flames? She might have a meltdown. Well, they both might have meltdown for real if they didn't get out of here soon.

"What's wrong?" she asked, then noticed the flames herself. She went white and started shaking.

"Wait there," Logan said. She wasn't going anywhere. She couldn't move.

He went to the inside door and yanked on it. It wouldn't budge. Meeka called out to him—she was holding out the spare paperclips she had made for picking the lock. Logan grabbed them off her and opened the door but there was a large bookcase blocking the entrance. His father had really had it in for them.

Logan pushed on it then shoved hard against it. It didn't budge. Jake must have jammed something between the bookshelf and the wall. They couldn't get out that way.

He ran to the other door—it was getting warm. He picked the lock and swung the door open. The heat tried to bowl him over as it rushed in the door. Across the path, the fire was getting taller and scarier. He wouldn't have a chance of getting Meeka to run up the stairs. He looked at her, desperation in his eyes. If any time was the time to pray, it was now, so he muttered out a few *Helps*. Abby sometimes made them go to church youth group, and the leader was always going on about how God was watching over them. He hoped that God had both eyes open tonight, because if he didn't think of something soon, Meeka and he would both be toast. Literally.

Out of the corner of his eyes he spotted the tarpaulin. Maybe there was something under there he could use to ram the bookcase. He yanked at the tarpaulin. No way! His dirt bike! He let out a shout. How did that get here? No matter—no time to think about it now. He took another look out the door and made out enough room to turn the bike round where the path widened by the bins. There'd be a bit of a run up from there too. Lucky he still had the key for his bike in his pocket.

Now to get Meeka to move when she was petrifyingly terrified. She had said something the other day—what was it? He crouched down beside her, and tried to speak calmly.

"Remember how you said you could play your piano to a crowd even though that would normally freak you out, as long as you imagined it was just you and your parents in a bubble?"

She focused all her attention on him, and nodded.

"I want you to imagine it's just you, me and my bike, and we're in a really large bubble. We're going to ride inside the bubble for a little bit, and when we stop, we'll get to see your parents." He looked at her, holding his breath, hoping his bubble babble would do it.

"Can I close my eyes? That always helps me imagine it better." She tried to smile at him, obviously exerting a lot of effort to try and control her panic.

"Sure. I'll tell you when. Here, put this on." He helped her into his helmet before she could change her mind. At least her hair wouldn't catch on fire.

He pushed the bike outside, and turned it around by the bins. Back inside, he forced Meeka out the door with a lot of yelling about bubbles and pulling on her arms. She climbed on the back and held him tight.

He had ridden up steep inclines with little kids before, but this was stairs, and Meeka wasn't a little kid. Not to mention the fire all around them. He was sweating as let the clutch go and powered towards the stairs. They hit the first one, bumping over it and going straight up.

He heard Meeka's scream even through the helmet. "We're going to die, we're going to die!"

He got to the top, swerved round the corner and stopped in front of the main door of the house. Made it! Relief washed over him as he turned around and grabbed Meeka's shoulders.

"We're all right, we're all right. We did it!" he yelled at her, lifting her visor. She stopped screaming and started thumping him on the head.

"Smoke, smoke. You're smoking!" She was laughing and crying all at once. Logan became aware of the pain in his head, and it wasn't from her hitting him. He whacked at his hair, too. They might not die, but that sure was going to hurt for a while. Meeka took her helmet off and inspected his head, like a monkey looking for fleas on its buddy.

## Chapter Twenty-Three:
## Gunshot

Cole's head was pounding and he saw and heard everything in slow motion.

"Shoot him," Oscar yelled, furious, as he nodded at Nate.

Alex started to bring his arm down to aim his gun at Nate.

Crack! A shot went off, ripping the air to shreds.

Cole tried to scream, but his throat was so tight, no noise came out.

Nate didn't fall down. *Why not?*

Cole turned his head to look at Alex. He was groaning and clutching his hand, which was bleeding everywhere.

The gun was on the floor.

Cole snapped out of his daze and leapt at the gun, kicking it out of the way. Nate ducked over to Poet, and pulled her back towards the window, away from Oscar and Zach.

A man sprang in from the veranda and went straight over to Zach, punching him in the face and knocking him unconscious. He turned towards Oscar and a savage fist fight broke out.

Nate pulled something out of his pocket. Powder bombs! That's what Logan and Nate had been so secretive about lately.

Nate threw the egg bombs hard at Oscar's back, one after the other. Oscar hesitated mid-punch, turning as a shower of talcum powder erupted all around him. Bet the boys had put pepper in there, too. That would sting! They'd got him with a powder bomb last summer and he could still remember how bad it felt.

The stranger took advantage of the distraction and landed two hard punches, one just below Oscar's nose and another to his temple. Oscar fell to the ground, out like a light.

It was all over in a few moments. Everyone went silent as they stared at the stranger, waiting for him to get his breath back.

Who was he?

Logan heard two shots explode the air. They were from inside the house! Maybe he was wrong about the not dying thing.

Meeka looked at him, shock on her face, the same shock he was sure would be echoed on his own face. He motioned for her to get down, and they crawled over to the window and peered inside. They could make out Cole, Poet and Nate slumped together with their backs to the window, all of them staring at something across the room, out of sight.

A thought elbowed its way into his mind. He looked at Meeka. The expression on her face said she was thinking the same thing.

"Fire," they chorused, as they ran to the door. Logan grabbed at Meeka's arm, slowing her down.

"Watch out for guns." They both stopped at the door— would they get shot if they charged straight in?

"That fire's going to catch onto the house any minute," Meeka pointed at the trees, her face desperate.

"We've got to get them all out," Logan said. They banged the front door open and ran inside.

## Chapter Twenty-Four:
## Not Over Yet

Cole could see from Nate and Poet's faces that they were bursting with as many questions about the stranger as he was. He was about to speak when the front door banged open.

"Fire! Fire!" Logan and Meeka ran into the room, shouting.

Meeka yelled out, ran up to the stranger and flung herself at him, hugging him hard.

"Come see the fire," she said and dragged him out onto the veranda and around the side of the house. Cole and the others followed. They all gasped when they saw the trees being swallowed up by the fire. The stranger pulled out his phone and made a call.

"You know how I called through for the police? We're going to need the fire department as well. Send a monsoon bucket too," he said.

After he hung up, he put his hands on Meeka's shoulders.

"Where are your parents, Meeka?" he asked.

"They're in Plymouth," she said. The man breathed out a long sigh and rested his forehead on the top of her head.

"I thought they might be lying bleeding to death somewhere," he said.

"Has anyone phoned them?" Cole asked.

"I sent Dad a text," Nate said. He checked his phone for a message. "They're on their way."

"Who *are* you?" Cole asked the stranger.

"I'm Andrew, Meeka's minder."

That's right—Cole remembered Meeka's parents talking about her minder when they were deciding whether she could stay at their place. He had mentally grouped Meeka's minder alongside nannies and babysitters when he was actually a bodyguard, and an expert marksman. Plus, he looked like Captain America.

"Let's get everyone outside," Andrew said, a frown appearing on his face as he glanced at the fire again.

"Who exactly are all you people? And what is going on?" asked Andrew as they dragged Oscar and Zach outside.

Cole introduced everyone then gave him a quick explanation, telling him about the coins being smuggled and the London guys down at the race-track.

"We need to get to the racetrack and stop those crooks from taking off," Logan said after Cole had helped Jake sit down on the grass. Cole noticed that Logan refused to look at his father. He must be gutted. His father was a criminal! And just when he'd finally started acting like he really belonged in their family. This better not set him back.

Cole cracked his knuckles as he looked around, frowning. "The fire department will be here any minute," he said, "then it's going to be crazy. If we're going to go, we need to go now. Logan could take his bike and I could use Alex's. Maybe you could take the others in the van, Andrew."

"Leave it to the police," Andrew said, his eyebrows meeting in the middle. "You think these guys are serious," he nodded at Oscar and Zach, who were now tied up in the middle of the lawn, "but I bet they'll be amateurs compared to the guys from London. If they're responsible for distributing those coins all across Europe, they'll be part of some organised crime syndicate. There'll be no discussion. It'll be shoot on sight."

Andrew headed inside to get Alex.

Cole glanced at Logan—had he even heard Andrew? "Don't try anything stupid Logan," he said.

"Come on Cole, those guys could get away. It's just not right. We could have all died. Someone should go and stop them. Mr MacAdden could create some kind of delay so they'd still be there when the police turn up."

"You heard Andrew. I bet he knows what he's talking about. The guys at the racetrack are dangerous," Cole lowered his voice and forced a smile. "Plus, I'm sick of being tied up." Would Logan drop it?

"I'm going to go talk to Andrew about it again," Logan said. Cole frowned as he watched Logan trail after Andrew, then he stepped over to look at Jake's leg. What a mess! At least Jake had tried to save Nate. Logan needed to know that.

"Quick, help Andrew!" Logan called out to him, and disappeared inside the lodge.

Cole ran up to the door and saw Andrew doubled over on the floor, clutching his head. A broken vase was scattered around his body. Judging by the pieces it had been big and heavy.

"Alex jumped me. I think he took off in the van," Andrew said. "Logan's gone off after him on his bike.

You'll have to go—I'm seeing double. Try and stop Logan, he'll get himself shot."

Cole ran out the front to Alex's motorbike. The key was still in the ignition, so he jumped on and raced after Logan.

## Chapter Twenty-Five:
## Smuggler's Captured

Logan didn't see the van between the house and the racetrack—Alex must have been rocketing. But as Logan skidded to a stop at the entrance to the track, he saw the van disappear behind a truck. It would be safer to ride a bit further down the road and climb through the hole in the fence he knew hadn't been fixed yet.

He found the spot, left his bike in the ditch, climbed through the fence and headed towards the garden shed. From there he could see what was happening.

Cole appeared at the entrance gate, stopped and looked around. Mr MacAdden waved to him from his office, and Cole rode over to him, got off his bike and yelled at him to put down the main gate barrier arm and put up the tyre spikes. Mr MacAdden frowned at him, but headed indoors to the gate control, asking what was going on.

A man stepped out of a car parked near the office and came up behind them. Hopefully not a guard posted by the racing guys?

He pulled out a gun and pointed it at Mr MacAdden. No!

"Best you ignore him, Mr Mac. If you want to see another day, that is. Inside, let's get you boys tied up tight."

Cole's going to be mad—tied up again. Hopefully that'll be the worst of it. What had Meeka's minder, Andrew, said? *It'd be shoot on sight with these guys.* Logan had to get them out of there before that man became impatient.

Maybe he could use something out of the garden shed. The door to the shed faced the side of the office. Logan saw the man's back leaning against the office window. If Logan was quick, the man wouldn't notice him. Logan pulled out the paper clips, unlocked the door to the shed and ducked inside.

Logan considered his options as his eyes grew accustomed to the dark. Next to the shed door was a small window, which let in a sliver of light. There was a large bush growing in front of the shed, covering most of the shed wall. Mr MacAdden had told him it stopped the shed looking like an eyesore from the office. He could hide behind that if he needed to.

"Paint tins … wheelbarrow … rope. Just need a sky hook," Logan whispered. Looking up, he saw a beam running across the centre of the shed. Perfect.

He tied a rope to the handle of a large paint tin, and threw the other end of the rope over the beam. He moved the wheelbarrow so it was under the beam, put the paint tin in the middle of the wheelbarrow, and threw the other end of the rope out the window. That should make enough noise.

Peering out the door, he saw the man still had his back towards the shed. Logan shot around the door, ducked behind the bush, and found the rope dangling out the window. He pulled on it, taking the weight of the full paint tin as it rose above the wheelbarrow. He let it drop.

Bang! Crash! He pulled on the rope again, raised the bucket, then let it drop again, and again. The man in the office peered out the window, looking frustrated at the noise. A minute later he stepped out of the office and marched over to the shed, cursing.

Once the man had stepped right inside the shed, Logan dived at the door, slamming it shut so it locked. He ran to the front of the office and stopped at the door to check the shed. Gunshots were going off as the man tried to shoot at the lock, but it wasn't working. Only in the movies!

A truck was speeding from the back of the complex towards the racetrack gate. The London guys were going to get away! Logan rushed into the office and pushed the buttons to activate the tyre spikes and the barrier arm. As the truck slowed down to go through the entranceway, it ran over the spikes, bursting its tyres.

Sirens! There were sirens approaching! Men jumped out of the truck, but they were too late. Three police cars swerved into the entrance and police officers swarmed out of the cars to apprehend the men. More police cars were driving into the racetrack from the back entrance, and they soon had everyone rounded up.

"What's going on?" Cole yelled. "Man, I am so sick of being tied up!"

Logan laughed and set to undoing him and Mr MacAdden.

Logan watched as another couple of police cars drove up not long later with the parents, Andrew, Nate, Poet and Meeka inside. They ran over to Logan and Cole, and swamped them with questions, hugs and slaps on the back.

All the parents were wiping their eyes and shaking their heads. They look like a set of those mechanical clowns at the fair—the ones that move their heads from side to side as customers throw balls in their mouths to try to win a prize.

Logan whispered that to Meeka and she snorted. "That would be a fantabulous image for Mum's next concert poster."

"Logan?" a sturdy looking man with grey hair apprpached him. "I'm Inspector Wright. I want to congratulate you on a job well done. If you hadn't got that man out of the office we could easily have had a hostage situation on our hands."

Logan felt his face heat up. "Thanks, it was nothing."

"You've got smarts and courage. Keep up the good work." Inspector Wright shook his hand then walked away.

Andrew and Cole both stared at Logan, their eyebrows raised and arms crossed. Cole turned to Andrew. "Do you think we should mention that the only reason that man had anyone *to* capture was because I was looking for a stupid kid who thought it was a clever idea to chase after the bad guy on a motorbike?"

Andrew shook his head. "Nah, I think we can forget that for now."

Logan's eyebrows gathered in and his faced flushed hotter. What could he say? Nothing. He looked at his feet. Andrew and Cole both laughed at him.

Cole punched him in his shoulder. "Come on, hero. We should go home."

"That's a good idea. You should all get out of here before any reporters arrive or you'll be hounded for weeks. I'll stay and talk to the police and make sure your names aren't given out to the press," Andrew said.

Steve and Abby came up to Logan and Cole and hugged them again.

"Let's get out of here," Steve said, his arm around Logan's shoulders.

# Chapter Twenty-Six:
# Lollapalooza

*Monday Late Evening*

Everyone was relieved to be home, to have the ordeal over. Abby and Steve found some food and drink for them because they were starving. Then the questions came and Steve made them tell their part of the story one at a time, taking turns until they'd pieced it all together.

Jason paced the room, getting more and more distressed as he listened. Abby and Lia's faces were set on horror mode as they sat next to each other, clutching each other's arms for support. Steve crouched, leaning against a wall. He looked ready to pounce on anyone coming through the door that might remotely resemble a baddie.

When Logan got to the part about the fire, Jason stopped pacing and stared at Logan, dismay written all over his face. Lia reached over and took his hand, her face stricken.

Now Logan started pacing the room, trying to keep the agitation out of his voice as he remembered the feelings of terror he'd had when he realised there was no way out of the room, and the fire could get to them any moment.

"So, I thought, maybe there would be something under the tarpaulin I could use to ram the door down, and I lifted it up and, whoa, there's my dirt bike." He stopped pacing and turned to Jason. "Do you know why that was there?"

"I bought it off Mr MacAdden for you, for a late birthday present. I didn't want to leave it in the garage because you might have seen it there. Janet suggested the basement because it was off limits. Makes sense now why Alex seemed so distressed—he insisted on putting it there by himself. Must have wanted to make sure Janet didn't see the buckets of coins," Jason said, shaking his head.

Logan looked at him, stunned. Jason had bought his bike for him. Was that all right? He turned to Steve and Abby. They smiled at him, letting him know with a look that it was okay with them.

Logan stared for a few moments more, and then shook himself. "Thank you Jason. That was one of your best ideas ever."

He continued his story, telling how they'd managed to use the bike to get out of the fire.

When he had finished, Lia hugged Meeka, and Jason held onto Logan long and hard. Then Steve and Abby had to have a turn. It was one big emotional scene, and nobody made a joke, not even Nate.

Logan looked out the window. A car was pulling up.

"What's that?" he asked, pointing. Meeka came over to take a look.

"It's the Bug. It'll be Andrew," she said.

"You mean Bugatti Veyron! That is so cool!" Nate said, his eyes wide open.

A Bugatti Veyron. What had the guy at the track said they were worth—nearly two million pounds? Meeka's minder was driving a Bugatti Veyron! You've got to be kidding! What did their cook drive?

Logan looked at Cole, and read his face. It said, "When I told you that they were from another planet, I meant, in another galaxy!"

After all that had happened, this was too much! Logan had to talk to Meeka.

He grabbed her by the arm and pulled her through the lounge and into the hallway.

"What's wrong, Logan?" Meeka's face was bunched up like a fist.

"I need to know whether Cole's right or not. When you get back to London, are you going to forget me and my family because we're so … so ordinary, and boring, and compared to you, we're flat broke?" He dropped his arm which he had been waving about as he had ranted, and stood there, shaking his head.

"Don't be stupid, Logan!" Meeka thrust her hands out, both palms open wide. "You just saved my life! Even if none of this stuff at the lodge happened tonight, I'd still think of you as my best friend."

She pulled out her mobile, then speaking a little quieter, handed it to Logan. "Look," she said. "Poet swiped your phone today while you and Nate were fooling around with the microwave pies and set me up as your Snapchat friend. I told her I wanted to Snapchat you in the middle of the movie to annoy you, but really I just wanted to make sure I could keep in touch with you, because …"

She looked up at the ceiling and went a little red.

"What?"

"Because I thought when I left, you might not want to bother being my friend seeing as I have oodles of money and no common sense. Lots of people give up on me because they think it's too hard to be friends with someone they can't keep up with. You know, with money and stuff." She stared down at her shoes.

"What?" Logan's mouth hung open.

Meeka looked up at him. "You look like one of those fairground clowns now."

He snapped his mouth shut. "This is crazy, Meeka. I think you're brilliant. Of course I want to be your friend. Here's the deal. You never wrote me off when you found out I had a loser for a father, so I won't write you off, either, especially not because you're rich!"

He glanced through the lounge at everyone sitting in the kitchen. Andrew had come in. "But we've got to have a code word to help me deal with your oodles of money. Some word I can say so you know when I'm sinking underneath all your gold. Then maybe you can help me not to drown."

He thought for a moment. "How about lollapalooza? I liked that."

Meeka smiled. "Okay, lollapalooza it'll be."

"Done. Well then, Meeka—lollapalooza!"

Meeka folded one arm across her stomach and put her other hand up to her face, index finger extended, head tilted to one side.

"What do you mean? What's bothering you?" she said, a slight frown on her face.

Logan sighed and shook his head. "It's like this. A few days ago, the most exciting person that ever sat at my kitchen table was Santa Claus. But that turned out to be Dad's workmate dressed up for the mid-year Christmas party. Now look!"

He pointed through the door towards the kitchen.

Meeka took a glance.

"Sitting at my table, right now, drinking cups of tea, are a famous mega-star *and* a famous stunt director. Normally, that would only partly faze me. But after being tied up, escaping a fire on my dirt bike and capturing a crook, I have to admit I'm finding it all a bit difficult to deal with. Especially since Captain America just drove up in a Bugatti Veyron!"

Meeka sighed and put her hands on Logan's shoulders.

"Calm down," she said. "Now, repeat after me, nice and slowly: famous people are just normal people who everyone watches."

He repeated it a couple of times while she nodded her approval.

"Now, about the Bugatti Veyron. Mum bought it for Dad for his birthday, but mostly Andrew drives it. He's been Dad's best friend for years, and since Dad's away so much, he gets to play with it. So don't stress about it. I don't even like it. Mum's is much better. It's pink with yellow flowers painted all over it."

"What!" Logan almost shouted.

Meeka laughed and thumped his chest. "You should see your face! Of course we don't have two Bugatti Veyrons. Only the splendi-ciously rich people have two. So you see, we're actually quite poor. You should be able to get along with us just fine."

Logan stared at the ceiling, then at her smiling face. "I'll remember that next time I run out of change at the school canteen."

"Yuk, who needs canteen food when you've got microwave pies in your freezer? You sure are one lucky kid!"

Abby popped her head round the corner. "You two coming back? Andrew's waiting for you before he'll tell us what he was doing here tonight."

"You right now, Cliffhanger?" Meeka asked. "Did I tie a knot in your rope in time to stop you slipping off?"

Logan laughed and put his arm round her shoulder. "Just in time, Captain Happy, just in time."

Andrew had grabbed a hot drink and was sitting down, cradling it in his hands.

"I rang you this morning, remember?" He turned to Lia. "Everything was fine, no problems, but I couldn't shake this bad feeling I'd had for a couple of days. So I decided I'd take the Bug for a spin and check up on you. I figured we'd have a laugh about my bad feeling, maybe go out to dinner and then I'd drive home again. But as I got close to the lodge, I saw this big guy standing at the gate, searching for someone. He looked like he was hiding a weapon under his jacket, so I drove on by and turned off the road around the corner. I grabbed my gun and sneaked back to see what was going on."

Andrew carried on, telling how he had seen Cole make a dash for it, then Nate and Poet get caught. He was obviously impressed with Cole's fighting skills, but hadn't wanted to make a move until he knew how many people he was dealing with, and where Meeka and her parents were. When Alex pointed his gun at Nate he had no choice. He shot the gun out of Alex's hand and jumped into the room. The rest of the story they all knew.

After that, Andrew wanted to hear their stories for himself so they started over again. This time when Logan finished telling about the fire, Meeka came over and gave him a hug.

"Thanks for saving my life," she said. Everyone else clapped and Logan went bright red in the face.

"The part I like best about it," said Nate, "is your hair. Your head looks like a munched-up chessboard!"

## Chapter Twenty-Seven:
## Figuring Things Out

*Tuesday Morning*

It was late when they finished talking. Cole moved into Poet's room for the night, surrendering his room to Jason and Lia. Meeka shared their room—she couldn't stop thinking about the fire.

In the middle of the night, Logan went searching for Nate and found him sitting in bed with Steve and Abby, talking about his 'getting shot' nightmare. Steve asked him if he was worrying about fires and he nodded sheepishly and crawled into their bed, too. First time he had ever done that. If it wasn't so squashed it would have been better, but he was so tired he soon fell asleep.

When Poet turned up in their room at seven in the morning, Steve was dozing on the floor. Logan heard him suggest to Poet they make pancakes, and then they left.

He wanted to roll over and stretch out, but his mum was lying next to him. Wicked. He had a mum! She'd looked pretty distressed about the fire—he'd thought she'd never stop hugging him. His heart sang at the memory, so he shut his eyes and let it lull him to sleep.

Thirty minutes later Poet was back, pulling off the blankets and interrupting his dream about driving a Ferrari made of pancakes.

"Come on guys, if you don't get down there soon, Jason and Andrew will gobble up all the breakfast," she said.

There was a lot of hanging around, waiting for the police to take everyone's statements. Janet was there as well, listening to everything. She kept shaking her head and muttering, "How could Alex do this? I just can't believe it."

The police had found out from Jake and Alex that someone had discovered a wreck and enlisted the help and financial resources of a mafia-like gang in London to pay for its salvage, in exchange for a share of any treasure discovered. They'd never had any intention of informing the Receiver of Wrecks. Instead they were planning on using their European money-laundering connections to convert the gold bullion into cash.

The police had informed the Royal Navy about the salvage ship's activities, and its captain and crew had been arrested.

The police told them Alex would be spending a number of years in prison, as would Logan's father. Tying up children didn't go down to well in a court of law, and neither did pointing a gun at kids.

That was too much for Janet. She stood up, tears streaming down her face and went outside. Abby followed to try and calm her down. Logan watched through the window as Janet hopped in her car and left, still distraught.

Logan walked outside to get some air. How was he supposed to feel about his father going to prison? It didn't rock him like Alex's arrest had rocked Janet. Mostly he was glad that he had a real home now—and a real family. He was sad about his father, but he couldn't feel the black cloud trying to suffocate him anymore.

He saw Poet sitting in the Bugatti Veyron by herself and went to join her.

She was staring into space. "You could have died, Logan Seagate."

"Maybe. I'm okay. Are you okay?"

She looked at him with tears brimming in her eyes. "I don't want you to die."

He stared at her for a few moments. "Are you crying for me?"

"Of course. What do you think I'm doing?"

"It's just … I was wondering, if it were me, not Cole that got caught, would you have been so pig-headed about rescuing me?"

Poet took a deep breath. "Nate said something when we were in the tunnel. He told me he was my brother, too, and it was like I suddenly saw that he, and you, were as important to me as Cole. I don't have one brother and two foster brothers; I have three real-deal brothers. So I think, yes, if it was you caught by those guys, I'd have been just as … determined."

Logan leaned back to soak in what she said, along with the feeling of luxury exuding from the Bug.

She smiled at him, put her feet on the seat and hugged her legs. "But do you even want a sister? I'm nothing special, after all. I can't even sleep through the night—it's like I'm stuck on baby mode. Maybe you'd rather have Meeka as a long distance sister than me as an at-home one."

"Poet, I've always wanted a sister, but I figured you were more Nate's sister than mine. You two have been friends so long. But if you can put up with me being a pain, I can put up with you being annoying. You'd be a great sister for me—I can so get you in trouble. Meeka would leave anytime the heat came down. Much better to have someone always available to take the blame."

Poet ricocheted his grin, before he added, "By the way, the seats in here are definitely a 'No Foot' zone. Just thought I should warn you before Andrew comes out."

"I wonder what would happen if I put my dirty toes on the windscreen," she said, lifting her feet.

"Whoa, I'm out of here. You live way too dangerously for me."

Inside, the police were talking about who the ringleader could be, as none of the men taken into custody would say who it was. It had to be someone with access to old sea charts and maps.

"I know," said Meeka. "It's Mr Gomander."

Cole rubbed his brow. "What? Why do you think that?"

"When I went to the bathroom at his house I played 'Notice' in one of his rooms. There was a white bucket like the ones in the van. It was against the wall, half hidden by this ugly rubbish bin in the shape of an elephant's head. He had some interesting stuff in that room, including maps and old-looking papers."

"Yeah, and he seemed to recognize the coins Cole showed him the other day," Logan said.

"Plus Oscar and Zach almost stopped at his house instead of walking past," Nate said. So he'd noticed that too. If only they'd talked about it.

"Maybe that's why I was so tired." Cole said. "I was the only one who drunk that juice remember? And then I couldn't keep awake afterwards. Maybe Mr Gomander put something in my drink."

Logan jumped up and paced the room. "He must have been trying to keep us away from the lodge, but then Nate told him we were going to be busy for the rest of the day, so he let us all go instead," Logan said. "Lucky none of the rest of us drunk that stuff or who knows what he'd have done to us."

This seemed to excite the police officers, who started talking search warrants. They took off in a hurry.

They got word a few hours later that Mr Gomander could not be found. All the maps Meeka had seen were gone, plus most of the coins from the walls and other valuables in the house. He had done a runner, but the police were sure they would track him down. Logan wasn't so certain. There was more to Mr Gomander than met the eye.

By mid-afternoon, the last of the police finished their questioning and drove away from Steve and Abby's, leaving everyone there feeling pretty flat and empty.

## Chapter Twenty-Eight:
## Another Get-Away

*Tuesday Late Afternoon*

Everyone sat down to work out what to do next. Logan figured Jason and Lia would want to head home—after all, Logan's home wasn't exactly a superstar-quality residence.

"We've had a great time staying here," Lia started off.

Logan rolled his eyes at the ceiling. *Here she goes. It'll be blah blah, have to get going, blah blah, shouldn't impose and blah blah, I really miss my mansion, my butler and my servant who irons my shoelaces.* He shook his head and let out a sigh.

Lia looked straight at him. "You sure are in a mood, Logan Seagate. When Meeka pulls a face like that there's only one thing to do."

Meeka's smile stretched wide across the room. "Let's go climbing!" she shouted.

Logan scrunched up his face. "What?"

Andrew looked out the window. "Here's Jed now."

Nate ran over. "Come and see guys! There's a flash Mercedes-Benz van pulled up. Some chauffeur-looking guy is hopping out!"

Noise exploded in the room like a bomb going off.

"Steve and Abby," Jason said, sounding firm, like he was talking to a stuntperson who was refusing to jump off a building. "We've made some plans, so it's no use you two arguing. You're all coming with us, so you may as well go pack a few things. If you argue you'll just make us late."

"He's right," said Lia. "We need to get out of Cawsand before the press figure out where we are. I've still got tomorrow off before I need to be back on the road on Thursday. I want to spend it with your family. But not here in Cawsand. Let's go check out the climbing place in Edinburgh."

Abby's mouth dropped open like the fairground clown again. "Edinburgh! How on earth will we get there?"

Jason looked at Lia. "You tell her," he said, smiling.

Lia put her finger across her chin. "In our private jet."

Abby looked stunned. "I think I'm going to faint." She shook her head, studied the ground for a half a minute, and then looked up, smiling.

"What are we waiting for? Let's go!"

After that, the day passed in a thrilling blur of

excitement. The ride to the airport, the flight in the private jet with an air hostess who doubled as hairdresser and dealt to Logan's checkerboard hair by giving him a trendy mohawk, the suite at the fanciest hotel in Edinburgh, the meal at the most exclusive restaurant, and the show at the theatre sitting in the best seats in the house.

### Wednesday

The next morning they went to the climbing complex. It was fantastic! Lia booked out the whole place. They each had an instructor to themselves, and everyone had a blast. Even Abby and Lia had a go, though Lia wasn't supposed to. If she hurt herself and had to cancel her tour she would be worse than up the creek without a paddle—she would be on the moon with no rocket back.

Meeka smirked and whispered to Logan, "She's bad like me. Doesn't like to be told what to do."

Meeka and Logan had a great time racing each other up the trickiest routes. Everyone else finished, needing a break, but they kept going while the others watched from the cafe. Finally, they too succumbed to aching arms and legs, and joined the rest of the group.

After lunch, Jason and Andrew took them all indoor go-karting, while Lia took Abby to the Royal Yacht Britannia. Lia wore a wig and big glasses, and looked completely different. Meeka looked at Logan.

"Unco-nerdo!" they said in unison.

"We'll see who's unco when I get to the go-karts later, you two."

Lia was right. After she returned and got into a go-kart, she zoomed past Logan and Meeka and finished way in front of them. Unbelievable! Jason would do anything for her—she must have had him rig her go-cart to get that far in front! That was so unfair!

Logan was going to give her a piece of his mind.

She was so far ahead though that she had already started talking to Cole when Logan parked and made his way over to her.

"I know you have difficulty with letting us in your world, Cole," she was saying, "because our money and my fame worry you, so I'd like a chance to prove I'm something apart from that. How about we do a deal? Five laps. I win, you try and forget the fame stuff. You win ... I don't know. You're not going to win so we don't have to think about that." She grinned and held out her hand for Cole to shake.

Logan came up to her right at that moment and stood, legs apart, hands on his hips. "Of course he won't win! You're nothing but a big fat cheat!"

She dropped her hand, turned to him and fumed, "I am not!"

She was too a cheat, and he was going to tell her. He opened his mouth, but she laughed and held up her hand for him to stop.

"Logan, you know what I love about you?"

What did she say?

More important, what was she going to say?

"It's that you got to know me a little before you found out I came along with fame and money. You just see me as Meeka's mum, and you treat me like any other mum, not like a superstar. Thank you. That's the best gift I've had in a long time." She gave him a big hug.

"We should adopt him," Meeka said, clutching her hands together and smiling.

"Afraid not, Meeka," Steve said. "He's not available."

Abby smiled at Meeka. "We're going to keep him."

"I don't know, maybe we could negotiate." Nate grinned. "How much would you be willing to pay for him? I can do you a deal and throw in our lawnmower as well."

Meeka's smile didn't hide her look of disappointment—
maybe she meant it for real—maybe she really did want her
parents to adopt him. What should Logan say? His words
felt all muddled like a bowl of alphabet soup.

He needed to tell her.

"Meek," he began, "I had a little sister once. Her name
was Dominica. Same as you."

Meeka gasped.

"She was killed in a car crash along with my mum. She
was four and I was six. I've always thought I would like
another little sister because I really wanted her back. But
once people die, they don't come back. No one can take her
place, not even Poet. The other day, you said I was your
best friend, and that's what I need—another best friend
besides Nate. You know, someone who prefers climbing
and motorbikes to being a ninja. What d'ya say? Can you
be my adrenaline buddy instead of my sister?"

Meeka was wiping tears from her eyes. Jason stepped up
and hugged Logan. "If we can't adopt you as a brother for
Meeka, we'll just have to adopt the lot of you as some kind
of family. Maybe nephews and nieces. How does that
sound?"

Cole interrupted. "Don't make promises to Logan you
can't keep."

Steve put his hand on Cole's shoulder, but Cole became even more agitated.

"Jason, you've got to understand that when someone close to you dies, it's like your heart's been blown up as big as a balloon, and then someone reaches in, yanks it out, and throws a thousand darts at it till it's ripped to shreds. And it takes a long time and a lot of love to put it all back together. Logan's heart had no chance to heal while he was with his father. It's only just beginning to get its shape back now, and it's mostly stuck together with lots of pieces of sticky tape. I don't want to see him hurt anymore, especially not by you promising a friendship you can't deliver on."

Logan looked at Cole, astounded. Cole loved him. He wanted to dance around Cole and chant, 'Cole really loves me, Cole really loves me'. Obviously, he was way too mature for that sort of nonsense so instead he basked in the feeling of the sticky tape slipping off his heart as another piece was sewn permanently into place.

There was a stunned silence. Cole turned around, leaned his forehead on Steve's chest, and groaned. "Did I just lose my rag at Jason Whitley and Lia Castenada?"

Abby came up beside him and put her arm round his shoulders.

Steve smiled. "Yes, oh great patient one, you did."

"That's extremely embarrassing, isn't it? Can you please help me disappear?" he asked.

"Cole, don't be embarrassed," Jason said. "You were right to be worried about how we could find time to keep our friendship going. Last night, after you'd all gone to bed the five of us—your parents, Andrew, me and Lia—spent a couple of hours hashing out how this whole friendship deal could come together. I think we came up with some pretty good ideas, so please stop worrying."

"That's right, Cole," Lia said. "After all you guys have done for us ... it's like the pages in your book have been glued into ours. Or, maybe, your flowers are growing in our garden ... or, your kite's tangled in our tree."

"Or better, your *tree house* is tangled in our tree," said Meeka, her eyes gleaming.

"Or, even better ... your Ferrari's kept in our garage," said Nate, his face hopeful.

Jason snorted, reached over, messed up Nate's hair then spoke to them all. "Don't mind Lia. She sings love songs for a living—sometimes it turns her brain to mush."

He winked at Lia who smiled at him.

Jason turned back to Cole. "I think what Lia is trying to say is that we're serious about making our friendship

The Trespasser's Unexpected Adventure

work—it's not an empty promise. We admire all of you, and we'd be honoured to be able to spend time with you." He held out his hand for Cole to shake.

Logan grinned as Cole shook Jason's hand. Hopefully Cole would stop worrying now—he should have known he could depend on Steve and Abby to sort it out with Jason and Lia. Ever since Steve had found Poet and Cole in that container all those years ago, they'd been totally protective of them both. Just like they'd been with him.

Poet came up and hugged Cole.

"You okay now, twit-too?" she asked.

Lia looked puzzled. "Twit-too?"

Cole frowned. "It's short for Wise Old Owl."

Lia and Jason looked at each other and laughed.

Lia put her hand on Cole's shoulder. "Twit-too, you still owe me a race. Are you in or not?"

Cole looked at her for a few moments.

"Eat my dust," he called out as he raced to the go-kart, Lia close behind.

Later that afternoon, Cole spoke with Logan alone, while they sat in the lounge.

"Sorry Logan, for giving you such a hard time about the Castenada-Whitleys," he said. "Seems I was wrong about them."

"You're right about most things. Guess you can't win them all," Logan said, smiling at him.

"I don't know about being right about most things. After all, I sure didn't pick Mr Gomander as a mastermind criminal." He stopped and stared at Logan, his face screwed up. "Come to think of it, you always said there was something about him you didn't like. How did you know that?"

"He made me uneasy. I didn't trust him. No real reason." Logan looked down at his feet. Confession time. "Actually, I had the coin-smuggling thing worked out before I lost my bike, but I didn't pay any attention to it. Guess I didn't trust myself. I wish I had. If I'd said something, we could have skipped the whole being captured and almost killed thing."

"Don't feel bad. I could've said something too. I just couldn't believe it either. We all survived. But hey, it looks like your gut feeling is way more accurate than my way of checking out people. How about if you pay more attention to your instinct next time, I will too?"

Logan gave a sigh of relief. "Okay, but don't feel bad about Jason and Lia. I'm glad you didn't trust them. Your balloon speech was out there brilliant. I'd of hated to miss out on that. Which, reminds me, I wanted to say something to you."

"What?"

"I'm only going to say it once."

"I'm listening."

Logan paused and took a deep breath. "Thanks. I love you, too."

Cole looked at the ground, then looked up and smiled at Logan. "You're all right, Logan Seagate. For a baby brother, that is."

"I'm not a baby!"

"Yeah, well your head looks like a baby's butt. Your mohawk is the crack."

Logan glared at him. Cole winked and punched him in the shoulder. Logan punched him back and they both burst out laughing.

# Chapter Twenty-Nine:
## New Beginnings

*Thursday*

"You never said lollapalooza once, Logan Seagate," Meeka said.

They were sitting in the Ferrari, waiting for Jason and Lia to finish saying goodbye to Steve and Abby. Andrew had already left in the Bug.

"A couple of times I almost did, but you were having so much fun. When that waitress kept offering to get me stuff at the restaurant I wanted to scream. I tried to lollapalooza you but you had your face stuffed in a serviette so she wouldn't hear you laugh."

"I think she really liked your haircut."

"Don't be stupid. She was showing off to your mum. Doesn't she ever get sick of people trying to impress her?"

"Yep. That's why she likes you so much. You're the most unimpressive person known to mankind."

Logan laughed, letting that one slide by. He borrowed a word from Meeka and said, "It's been an astounda-mungus brilliant time Meeka, but the bit I'll remember most of all is when my sad dribbled out my toes. I still owe you a couple of splashes, so you better come back sometime so I can drench you thoroughly. What d'ya say?"

She looked at him, the smile in her eyes reminding Logan of her dad. He was going to miss them all, even Lia, who'd proven she was so much more than a mere singer. Man, she was fast behind a wheel. Cole hadn't stood a chance.

"I reckon we need a couple of practices in my swimming pool. So maybe you should come up for a weekend or something before the next holidays."

"Of course, you would have a swimming pool. Don't tell me it's indoors."

"Yep, it's huge and it's heated. I practice rolling my kayak in it."

"Huh. I guess you have an even bigger one for actually swimming in."

"Twitiot. You'll just have to come and see."

He sure hoped he would. Maybe they'd come pick him up in the jet again. Or the Bug. Now that would be fine-tuned fabulous!

In the middle of the night Logan heard Poet stumble into the bedroom. Poor Nate. He was fast asleep. He probably had no new jokes even if Poet did manage to wake him up.

Suddenly two big eyes appeared at the top of the ladder.

"You awake?" Poet whispered.

"Yep, but I dunno any jokes." Logan sat up and leaned against the wall, and she climbed up and sat beside him.

"Shame."

"But I have been thinking up a story for the last half an hour. It features a Bug, a platypus, two sticks of dynamite, and a peanut butter sandwich. Do you want to hear it?"

"It doesn't have any kissing, does it?"

"Yuk, no," Logan said, almost forgetting to whisper.

Nate lay there, pretending to sleep as he listened to the story, finding it hard not to laugh aloud at the funny bits. As it came to the end, he smiled to himself. It'd been a long time since the day he had dragged Logan out of Jake's place. Finally, Nate could stop worrying. Logan had found his way home.

# Thank You For Reading!

Dear Reader

I hope you enjoyed *The Trespasser's Unexpected Adventure* and getting to know Logan, his foster family and friends. when Logan and his family will visit Meeka at her mansion-home and find not only wealth, but secrets, danger and ninja socks.

If you are interested, you can read the prequel to the Crime Stopper Kids Mysteries Series for free when you sign up to receive my newsletter at my website (www.karencossey.com). The Runaway Rescue is the story of Cole and Poet and how they came to live with Nate, Steve and Abby. Keep an eye out for a younger Logan too!

As an author, I love inventing stories that you will enjoy reading, that touch your heart and make you want to read more. So please tell me what you liked, what you loved, even what you hated. I'd love to hear from you. You can write me at: karen.cossey@gmail.com, visit me on the web at www.karencossey.com, find me on Instagram @KarenCosseyWriter or like me on facebook here: www.facebook.com/KarenCosseyAuthor. Plus I enjoy making book pins about my stories for Pinterest at KarenCosseyAuthor (I could get lost on there for hours!).

Finally, I need to ask you a favour. If you want to, it will mean a lot to me if you could take a few minutes to write a review of *The Trespasser's Unexpected Adventure*. Reviews make such a difference to other readers knowing whether they would like a book—you can help others to discover stories they would enjoy as much as you do. If you bought your book from Amazon, here's a link to the book page for *The Trespasser's Unexpected Adventure:*

### *http://viewBook.at/amazonstores*

Scroll down to the Customer Reviews section. On the left side is a button "Write A Customer Review". If you click on that you'll be taken to a page where you can share your thoughts (you will have to login if you haven't already done so).

Thanks so much for reading *The Trespasser's Unexpected Adventure* and for spending time with the Crime Stopper Kids. See you again at Meeka's place!

Until then,

Happy Reading!

Karen Cossey

# Acknowledgements

The Trespasser's Unexpected Adventure wouldn't have been finished without the perseverance of my husband, Peter, my strongest critic and biggest fan. Thank you for all your love, encouragement and support. For understanding my hours at the computer and distractedness at the dinner table, I also thank my awesome children, Daniel and Amy.

My sincere gratitude goes to Iola Goulton for her professional advice and assistance in editing The Trespasser's Unexpected Adventure. Thank you for everything you taught me.

Amanda Swanepoel, you were a delight! You're unshakeable belief in what I was doing helped pick me up, dust me off and put me back on track many times. I'll be forever grateful; thank you.

Jean Anderson, your proofing and comments were insightful and invaluable; I treasure your support. Etheljoy Smith, your belief in me and my writing kept me going.

Melanie, your enthusiasm to read my first draft was refreshing and your comments were more than helpful.

Others who taught me included Brent Martin, who took me abseiling and sent me over the edge. Thanks for keeping me safe! The professional insights of Rose Cherringon, a retired constable with NZ Police, helped me to shape the fighting scenes. Thank you so much for your excellent contribution Rose.

I couldn't have come up with the ideas of the motocross tricks without Phil Falconer's input. Shane Harrison, I look forward to one day racing in a Ferrari with you! Alright, maybe we'll just end up watching someone else race in a Ferrari, but it's nice to dream...thanks for all your petrolhead advice.

# Glossary

Anchor:

An arrangement of one or (usually) more pieces of gear set up to support the weight of a belay or top rope

Belay:

To protect a roped climber from falling by passing the rope through, or around, any type of friction enhancing belay device. Before belay devices were invented, the rope was simply passed around the belayer's hips to create friction.

Barn-door:

If a climber has only two points of contact using either the right or left side of their body, the other half may swing uncontrollably out from the wall like a door on a hinge.

Chauffeur:

A person employed to drive a private vehicle or limousine for the owner.

Curmudgeonly:

Bad-tempered, difficult, or cantankerous.

Dan:

A black belt degree of expertise in martial arts, e.g. A 2$^{nd}$ dan is the next level after 1$^{st}$ dan black belt in taekwondo.

Discombobulating: Confusing or upsetting.

Flagging:

Climbing technique where a leg is held in a position to maintain balance, rather than to support weight.

Incognito: In disguise

Lollapalooza:

An extraordinary, exceptional or unusual thing, person, example or event.

Minted: To make coins by stamping metal

Nac Nac:

A freestyle trick in which the rider brings one leg over the seat and then puts his foot back on the peg for the landing.

Omnium-gatherum: A miscellaneous collection.

Rappel (or Abseil):
The process by which a climber can descend a fixed rope.

Schnook: An unimportant or stupid person, a dope.

Superman:
A freestyle trick where the rider keeps his hands on the grips and straightens his body and legs above and parallel to the bike.

Whip:
Freestyle trick in which rider lays the bike flat horizontally in the air and then brings it back up for the landing.

Source of climbing terms:
http://en.wikipedia.org/wiki/Glossary_of_climbing_terms
Source of motocross terms:
http://www.motoxschool.com/mxtermscopy.htm

# A Free Gift For You

## Book Two of the Crime Stopper Kids Mysteries

## The Con Artist's Takeover
### *The Mystery of the Unco-Nerdo School Teacher*

Meeka has a secret that scares her into silence,
a burden she can't even trust with her friends.
All Logan, Nate and Poet want to do is help her,
but when they uncover a crime,
Meeka acts like she wishes they weren't there.
Will they have enough loyalty and courage
to not only solve the mystery
but save their friendship…and their lives?

**Find out more at http://viewbook.at/amazonbookshop
or read the first three chapters
FOR FREE (in digital format)
when you sign up to Karen's newsletter at:
www.KarenCossey.com/Newsletter/**

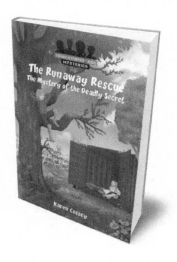

# The Adventures of Crimson and the Guardian

*A Medieval Children's Story for 8-10 year olds*
*full of Unicorns, Dragons and Magic!*

Crimson, the last of the elusive unicorns, steps into young orphaned Kinsey's path and life. Within minutes Kinsey finds herself battling a huge and dangerous river monster with nothing but a magical cloak and a dagger. Somehow she survives, and with her sense of adventure awakened, she agrees to travel with Crimson on an incredible journey towards more danger than she could ever imagine.

At every encounter Kinsey discovers more about the cloak's magic secrets and surprises herself with her own abilities. *But has she learned enough to be able to defeat the deadliest enemy of all, the Pegasus of Peril?*

**Find out more at http://getbook.at/amazononline**
**or read the first three chapters**
**FOR FREE (in digital format)**
**when you sign up to Karen's newsletter at:**
**www.KarenCossey.com/Newsletter/**

# FREE BOOK: Cinderella Sarah—Short Stories for Kids

***Bedtime Stories for Children, Fun Classroom Read Alouds and Short Stories For Kids.***

Find all sorts of fun read aloud children's yarns and heart-warming bedtime stories for kids ages 4-8. There are fairy tale characters, pets, school friends, angels, dinosaurs, monsters, and dragons! It's one of those fun books for kids you'll enjoy as much as your child or student!

**Receive the complete book
FOR FREE (in digital format)
when you sign up to Karen's newsletter at:
www.KarenCossey.com/Newsletter/**

Made in the USA
Monee, IL
01 July 2020